WELCOME
TO THE
MAZE

A Novel

By

Charles Truth

Printed in the United States of America

ISBN 1-4251-0421-5

Published by: CHARLES TRUTH

Emai: charlestruth@hotmail.com
Edited by: Carla M. Dean for U Can Mark my Word

Cover design: Jermaine "Jae One" Jude of Urban Nerd Studios llc. get@jermainejude.com
Cover Model: "rap artist" Analiza Slim

This book is dedicated to
Qutice Cole McGaughy a.k.a.
Colfax Cac
Rest In Paradise, bro.
1800

I can remember clearly. I was in the heart of the streets. I knew a pimp who was prayin' to preach and a dopeman that couldn't stay in the reach of any law. A dopefiend turned out, a man that done so many years in jail he got burned out. A black woman in a black dress and hat had a son who was a gangbanger. Death didn't surprise her. Streetwalker disappeared without a trace of her blood. A working man done gone mad and started taking some drugs. A young nigga pulled the trigga held a high school hostage; he was raised inside a broken home and couldn't make it to college. A crack baby on a respirator fightin' for its life. His daddy died inside an alley while gettin' high on the pipe. Housewife with AIDS; hubby trickin' money for thrills. When he ain't home, she in the bathroom swallowin' pills. A black man on the corner in a suit with a fade, promoting Mecca for a shekel in the heart of The Maze...

Most of us get trapped inside, but some do manage to find their way out!

CHARLES TRUTH

THE SEED
OF
CONFUSION

CHAPTER 1

It was August 12, 1980, sometime around eleven o'clock p.m. on a Thursday. He began to kick harder until she finally acknowledged the sharp pain he was causing in her stomach. She was nine months pregnant with her son, and she knew it was about time for him to make his entrance and see what the world was all about. Everybody thought she was trying to fool them when she told them that she was going into labor.

Friday the 13th at 12:01 a.m., Raekwon was born into a broken home. His mother knew he was going to be a problem child by the trouble he gave her when she was trying to push him out. Just four months before he was born, she came to Denver, Colorado, from Memphis, Tennessee, to visit her aunt. When she got there, she fell in love with the state and decided to stay. She couldn't even afford a baby picture of her son, and his pops said the baby was too bright-skinned and Chinese-looking to be any child of his.

There Raekwon was, his mother's second child, with no direction in life. Damn near everybody that his mother hung out with, including her cousins, were alcoholics, hustlers, dopefiends, and con artists. He became a product of his environment, not really aware or even knowing he would only grow up to be what he learned to be, which was what he was seeing and hearing around him. Raekwon started moving fast and learning fast, and by the age of three, he was cursing out all of the kids on the block, stealing, and roaming a two-block radius without supervision.

His household was violent. One of his mother's boyfriends knocked her front tooth out in front of him and his older brother. He was the same person responsible for teaching Raekwon how to cuss. That was the last woman's tooth he ever knocked out because he found himself waking up under an unpleasant fountain of scorching hot water that was fresh off the stove. They never saw him again.

By the time Raekwon turned four years old, he had learned how to play with fire and got burnt, literally. As usual, he found one of his mother's lighters and began roaming the rundown, drug-infested home in search of some roaches that he could paralyze and burn up.

He stepped on the back of a roach that had come from underneath a chair in the living room. He got on his knees to get a little closer to the action as he flicked the lighter aflame. When he turned the lighter upside down, the flame also turned upside down, and to his surprise, it burned the living shit out of his thumb. He dropped the lighter and sucked his thumb as the taste of his burnt fingernail put an unpleasant taste in his mouth.

After his thumb cooled off, he picked the lighter back up, curiously gazing at it as he rotated it, and noticed a lever on the back of it. He pushed the lever to the far right and flicked the lighter only three or four inches away from his face. The enormous flame jumped out at him, and before he had a chance to react, his hair was on fire and he was running towards his mother's room.

That experience should've set Raekwon straight, but several months later, sometime after he turned five years old, he ended up setting a building on fire with some of the other hoodlums in the neighborhood that he ran with. That was the inception of his criminal record.

Early one morning in 1985, his mother's cousin, Faye, was in town from St. Louis. His mother stayed out all night and didn't come home the following morning. Her cousin was in the living room on the couch asleep. Raekwon and his brother would usually eat generic brand Honeycomb cereal that came in the black and white box. Their mother would fix it for them every morning.

When Raekwon tried to wake Faye up to make them some cereal, she said in a very disturbing manner, "I'll be up in a minute!"

That minute turned into fifteen minutes. Growing impatient, Raekwon told his brother to go wake her up. She gave him the same response, and that's when they both began to get angry. Raekwon prepared himself for the unthinkable as he told his brother what he was getting ready to do.

He waited for ten more good minutes to make sure she was nice and comfortable in her sleep. He tiptoed over to the couch, climbed on the arm of it, and pulled out his little dick. He glanced over at his brother with a devious smile on his face and then stared back at his target. When he began to piss all over her face, she hopped up faster than a gang member getting shot at and shoved him off of the arm of the couch. She beat his little ass until his cries started sounding like a cigarette smoker's cough.

When his mother got home and found out what had happened, she damn near beat the black off of him, too. He never did anything like that ever again, but he enjoyed the moment of laughter he got from it.

He never really thought about things before he did them because the consequences were never anything he hadn't already suffered and stood through. He was too young to care or know anything about respect.

His mother used to always call him a mannish little bastard, and for that simple fact, all of the other grownups called him that, too. Obviously, the character of being young and mannish grew on him because he did a lot of mannish things as a kid.

He remembered stealing twenty dollars from his mother and taking it for Show & Tell in kindergarten. The only thing he didn't tell his teacher was the truth. He then somehow ended up showing the girls in his class his little nuts and got himself into some deep trouble over it. It resulted in his mother coming up to the school and whooping his young, black ass in front of his classmates since he wanted to steal her money, pull out his nuts, and then get mad and start flipping over tables.

He began to grow up and focus on the more essential things in life, like hustling to get what he wanted. His first hustle was the charm of being a kid who wanted something from anybody. He was able to come up on a dollar a piece from damn near every drunk and hustler that he could con out of it. He had his usuals that would break bread every time they saw him, and then he had to deal with those people who made him work for that dollar bill.

Soon, he got his first dub on a sack of dope. He was so young when he started that the dopefiends wouldn't cop from him, because to them, he was just a baby.

Raekwon was just a young, poor hustler trying to make ends meet. In the streets was where he learned principles, codes, and oaths. He wanted to be somebody that was important, so that's what he set out to do and wasn't going to let anyone stop him. He learned a lot from the streets, and one of the things he learned how to do by the age of fifteen was save enough money to purchase him a vehicle.

CHAPTER 2

It was an extremely hot day in late June. It was 1995, and Raekwon was fifteen years old. He had just bought a 1980 Regal in the late part of the previous month. The car had no back bumper and the catalytic converter was shot, if it even had one because he never bothered to check and see. He was fine with the car's condition, though, since he had only paid three hundred dollars for it. That was money he had hustled in the streets for, and it went as fast as it came.

He was on his way to the liquor store with this dopefiend named RoRo, when he spotted a cool little broad walking by Silverman Park. He slowed down and pulled up beside her. She was a pretty red-bone with smooth skin and had on some tight-ass daisy dukes. She wore a fake ponytail, but her full lips and sexy walk made up for it.

He asked, "What's up?"

"What's up?" she answered back in a sassy voice, as if she was frustrated.

As he asked her name, she wiped the sweat from her forehead. She told him that her name was Shae and that she had just moved to Colorado from Texas. It couldn't be denied that she was from down south by the shape of her nice, round ass. She had a sexy southern accent, too. Since she didn't act standoffish, Raekwon took it to mean that she was interested in him.

He asked her if she had a number he could call her at sometime in the future. She seemed hesitant with the presence of RoRo, but he could tell she didn't want him to notice her discomfort. She reached inside the small purse hanging from her shoulder and pulled out a purple pager. She scrolled through the pager as if she was looking for a particular number.

She stared at the pager's screen, then smacked her juicy, gloss-covered lips and asked, "You ain't gonna give my number out, is you?"

"Naw, girl, I promise," he quickly replied, while giving her a sincere look.

"Well, my daddy be trippin'. So, I'ma give you my pager number."

He told her that was cool and that he would call her soon.

Seeming concerned, she asked, "When?"

He gazed at her in thought and then replied, "I'ma keep that a secret, but my code is 303."

With that out of the way, he pulled off.

Even though it only took seven or eight minutes to knock that broad, it felt like the inside of the car was going to roast him in the process since he had no air conditioning. He leaned his left elbow out the window as he pulled off and the breeze began to kick back in. RoRo looked at him and started laughing.

"What?" Raekwon asked in a high-pitched voice and with a concerned expression on his face.

"You think yo' lil' ass got game, huh?" RoRo exclaimed.

Raekwon sat back. "Nigga, you ain't seen shit yet. I just let that lil' bitch off easy 'cause it's hot."

RoRo was a cool dude, but the only thing was Raekwon knew that dope would make him do almost anything. They always saw things eye to eye, and Raekwon never tried to get over on him as long as RoRo gave him the same respect.

They pulled up to the liquor store shortly after the conversation. The police were sitting in the parking lot of the car wash that was across the field. Having a little over a gram of crack on him, Raekwon was trying to be cautious. He was spooked as a roach in a rundown kitchen when the lights turned on. So, he took the dope sack out of his right pocket while coming to a screeching stop.

"What the fuck is you doin' actin' paranoid?" RoRo asked. "Them muthafuckas ain't payin' us no attention."

Truthfully, Raekwon didn't know if they were looking at them or not since he was always told to never look at the police when you're in the car because it would arouse their suspicion, which may cause you to get trailed and pulled over.

Raekwon lifted up off the seat and stuffed the sack of dope in the crack of his ass.

"Fuck that shit!" he told RoRo. "I ain't paranoid. I just ain't about to catch no dope case. My tags is expired, and I'm too young to be drivin' any muthafuckin' way!"

RoRo looked at him as if he was concealing his frustration. "Just calm down. It ain't even that big of a deal. Now, what is you tryin' to get out of this liquor sto'?"

Raekwon reached deep into his right pocket and pulled out a wad of crumbled and folded bills, which amounted to about one-hundred and seventy-eight dollars after he counted it. He sat for a moment trying to figure out what he wanted other than a case of 16-ounce Old English that he and the homies drank on the regular. Raekwon finally decided he wanted a personal half pint of Hennessy.

While Raekwon handed over enough money to cover the bill, RoRo looked at him with a wrinkled face of concern and asked, "You ain't gonna buy me a beer?"

Raekwon looked at him like he asked a stupid-ass question, which in his opinion it was. He handed him two more dollars, then cut his eyes at him to let him know he better not cross that line.

As RoRo stepped out of the car and went into the liquor store, Raekwon leaned back in his seat. He had a couple of big-ass doobies in the ashtray, so he grabbed one and fired it up. He had just started back smoking weed, but only in small doses because six months prior, in December of '94, he had a real bad experience with weed…at least the weed he smoked that day.

***

Raekwon was down in his homeboy Kel's basement with him and LP. They'd just bought a twenty sack of some light-green, skunk-looking shit from the people next door that drove the yellow Cadillac with the white fender.

They always bought the big-ass King Edward blunts in the glass tube so they could use the glass tube to rock up the crumbs from their dope sacks because the dopefiends loved re-rock.

They put the whole twenty sack in the blunt like usual and started playing a dank game called "Yellow Cloud." The object of the game was to hit the blunt so hard that they inhaled a thick, yellow cloud. Then they had to hold the smoke in until the blunt came back around, or you would get punched in the chest.

After the blunt came around to Raekwon for about the fifth time, he unexpectedly grew strange with his actions. It appeared to him that his heart rate sped up. So, he stood up real fast, put his right hand on his chest, and turned down the music.

Raekwon then looked at Kel and LP with a crazy expression and said, "My muthafuckin' heart is beatin' fast than a muthafucka!"

Raekwon was standing right in front of Kel's waterbed. He thought he was hallucinating when it started to wave because he got dizzy and plopped down into his seat. Immediately, he stood back up and put his right hand on his throat.

"My throat is dry than a muthafucka. I think I need some water," he told them.

They all went upstairs and into the kitchen, where Kel grabbed a cup and filled it with water. When he handed him the cup, Raekwon attempted to take a drink, but instead of putting the cup up to his mouth, it seemed as if his hand had a mind of its own because he ended up tossing half of the water over his shoulder. Raekwon implied he didn't do it on purpose and that he didn't know how it happened.

Kel and LP looked at Raekwon in suspense after realizing he was being serious. He quickly put the cup down and rushed outside. LP followed closely behind him, while Kel watched from the door because he was on house arrest. The nice, mild wind blowing across Raekwon's face felt good.

LP asked, "Is you alright?"

"Yeah," Raekwon replied. "All I needed was some fresh air."

As they stood on the sidewalk in front of Kel's house, all of a sudden he was struck with another burst of hallucination. So, they started to walk off. LP followed Raekwon, while telling him if he drank some of the forty ounce of Old English that was in his hand, it would probably calm him down. Raekwon rejected his offer while continuing to his house, which was only around the corner.

When they reached Raekwon's house, they went in the back door and down the stairs. Raekwon went into his room in search of something, but had forgotten what he was looking for as he rumbled through a drawer full of papers. He finally remembered he was looking for his little orange pocket-bible, as he stumbled across it in the drawer. He grabbed the bible, walked back into the common area, kneeled down in the middle of the floor on the carpet, and began flipping through the pages with no sense of direction.

"What you lookin' for, homie?" LP asked.

Raekwon closed the bible and stood up. "I don't even know."

He ended up giving his hundred and something dollars in dope to LP and told him to get out of his momma's house. Raekwon then went upstairs to wake his mother and stepdad. They thought he was on LSD, even though he told them that he had only smoked a little bit of weed. His stepdad tried to get him to go outside with him, but he kept sprinting back to the room where his mother was because he thought she was an angel.

That day, he learned a hard lesson. Stay clear of suspicious people that move into the neighborhood just to get their hustle on. It all boiled down to knowing who he was dealing with.

***

As Raekwon sat back in the car in a daze, RoRo came walking out of the liquor store with his arms full of the items that Raekwon had requested. He took the keys out of the ignition and hopped out of the car, while pulling up his pants to keep them from falling too low. Raekwon walked to the trunk and popped it open.

RoRo asked, "Why you puttin' this shit in the trunk?"

"'Cause I don't want the police to trip wit' a nigga if they pull me over after I drop you off," he responded confidently.

"Nigga, if they pull yo' ass over, all you gonna do is get out and run anyway," RoRo exclaimed, with his eyes cocked open and his mouth revealing his missing tooth.

"I don't feel like runnin' from them muthafuckas today 'cause I'm sore from hittin' fences on they ass yesterday," Raekwon told him.

RoRo grinned as he put the case of sixteen ounces of Old English in the trunk. He held on to the bag that contained his beer and Raekwon's Hennessy. The police were gone from where they had been parked, so he wasn't tripping off of them anymore. With it still hot, he hurried up and pulled off so he could get into the wind.

He pulled up at RoRo's house to drop him off. His pager had been going off, so he asked RoRo if he could use his phone. That's when Raekwon noticed he was staring over at the other side of the street for some reason. When he glanced across the street, he recognized the dopefiend broad named Cheryl that RoRo ran the streets with. She was in the passenger seat of a raggedy-ass yellow Datsun pickup truck with a white man that he had never seen before.

Raekwon gave RoRo a confused look and asked, "Who the fuck is that with that bitch Cheryl?"

"Don't even trip, man," RoRo replied. "He's a regular spender, but I ain't never brought him around you 'cause I know you don't like to meet new muthafuckas."

RoRo got out of the car and signaled for Cheryl to meet him in the house. When they got inside, RoRo and Cheryl went into the bathroom. When he came out of the bathroom, he walked into the kitchen where Raekwon was waiting for him to bring him the cordless phone. RoRo had a hundred dollars in his hand that the white man in the truck wanted to spend, and of course, he wanted his portion for making the sale for Raekwon. He decided to give RoRo the rest of the dope he had on him, which was about one-hundred and forty dollars' worth.

Raekwon smacked his lips and asked, "Nigga, is you gonna bring me the phone or what?"

"Yeah, man, just a minute. Let me go get a quick hit of this. It ain't even gonna take five minutes," he responded.

RoRo had to be about thirty-five years old and still lived with his mother, who was never really home to know he was smoking dope in her house. His mother would always lock the phone in her room, but he would get a butter knife to pop the door open when she wasn't there.

When Raekwon finally got the phone in hand, he scrolled through his pager and realized his homie Carlos had been paging him from a number he didn't recognize. He knew it was him because of the code used. When Raekwon called him back, Carlos told him that he was down the street from his crib getting high with one of his neighbors, and he wanted Raekwon to meet him at his house to pick him up. After telling him that he was on the way, Raekwon hung up.

Raekwon knew the beer that was in his trunk was getting hot and flat, so he yelled down into the basement to tell RoRo that he was leaving. He peeked into the refrigerator to see if RoRo's mother had some of those cold sodas that she kept on the regular. He saw two cans of Pepsi hiding behind a big pot of leftover collard greens that smelled like they had been sitting in there since Christmas.

Raekwon took one of the Pepsi's and put it in his pocket. Then he gently closed the refrigerator door and made his way across the squeaky kitchen floor. When he got to the front door, he was glad to get a whiff of fresh air. Their house smelled like an old-folks home that was full of wet clothes and rotten vegetables. Not to mention the fact that they had an elderly Doberman Pincher that ran around the house taking a shit everywhere.

After pulling up to Carlos' house, he turned off the car and went up to the door. Right before he had a chance to knock, Carlos opened it, signaled for Raekwon to come inside, and then walked towards the kitchen as he talked on the cordless phone with a grin on his face.

Curious as to who was on the other end, Raekwon pointed at the phone and whispered, "Who's that?"

Carlos was a real cool dude, who kept a list full of broads in his wallet and a pocket full of condoms in case he needed them. Raekwon was never surprised to see him with a different broad. The thing about Carlos was that he was the only Mexican Raekwon knew that only messed with black broads, and was serious about it. Nobody could tell him shit about a bitch. Let him tell it, he already knew. He had the same mentality as the

23

rest of them, and that's just how they treated him.

Carlos hung up the phone with a big grin on his face.

"What's up wit' that broad you was hollering at?" Raekwon asked.

"That bitch said her mom is goin' to Central City to go gamble and she want some niggas to come over there tonight. She got two friends, too."

Raekwon stroked his chin. "Where you meet that broad at?"

"Shit, I met her the other day when I took my mom's car to that car wash over there by the 7-11." He gazed off as if he was contemplating and then continued. "I hopped out of the car and my eyes damn near popped out of my head. I waited for the bitch to come out of the store, and I threw my hands up at her to get the hoe's attention."

"Oh yeah?" Raekwon responded.

"Yeah." He sat down and continued. "The broad threw her hands back up at me, so I walked over to her car. She tossed her fruit punch through the car window onto the seat, and waited for me to walk up. When I hollered at her, she seemed like she was down wit' whatever. She had hella ass on her, too."

"That's cool, homie. I met a lil' broad today, too, so niggas should have somethin' to get into later on," Raekwon told him.

After they finished discussing their plans for later, they went and hopped in the car. Raekwon reached in the back seat to grab his Hennessy, but it wasn't there. He immediately started up the car and headed back to RoRo's house.

When they pulled up to RoRo's, he was sitting on the porch drinking the beer Raekwon bought him. He got up and grabbed the brown paper bag that was next to him.

"I knew you was coming back sooner or later," RoRo said,

while walking over to the car.

Raekwon had been so busy trying to sneak out with the soda that he had forgotten his Hennessy. As soon as RoRo handed him the bag, he removed the bottle and opened it up.

"I don't know how you young muthafuckas drink hard liquor in this hot-ass weather," RoRo commented, "but it's gonna catch up wit' y'all one of these days."

Raekwon paid him no mind as he put the car in drive and told him to hit him later.

RoRo always kept Raekwon's pockets healthy. He was a hustling-ass dopefiend. It didn't matter if it was hailing outside. He would still be blowing up Raekwon's pager and knocking on his basement window. If he missed calling Raekwon for a day, it was only because he was in jail or something more serious.

Raekwon passed the bottle he thought would be a personal share to Carlos as they pulled off. Carlos loved to drink just as much as Raekwon, so they had no problem having fun. Since neither had no idea where they should go, they decided to just slide through the blocks of the town that they referred to as The Maze.

After hitting a couple of blocks and seeing niggas, broads, dopefiends, and children, they finished the bottle of yak and wanted something to get into. It so happened Raekwon decided to hit the block he lived on and saw an Asian dopefiend outside of his house fertilizing his grass.

One of Raekwon's homies and his cousin beat the shit out of the man one day for going over to their house and asking them for some dope right in front of their grandmother. The messed up part is that they had already warned him to never come to the house. Sometimes these are the things dopefiends do for that dope. He ended up leaving with a black eye and a couple of bruises, and the police ended up at the homeboy's house. The homeboy Ty didn't take no shit from dopefiends even as a young nigga, and they ended up giving him an assault charge.

Now, when Raekwon saw the Asian dopefiend, he got on some gangsta shit knowing that he was the reason his homeboy Ty might have to go do some time in jail.

When Raekwon pulled in front of his house and demanded that he come to the car, the Asian had the nerve to tell him to hold up and continued to do what he was doing.

"Don't make me get out of this muthafuckin' car and beat yo' ass!" Raekwon said with a vicious look of assurance on his face to let him know he was serious.

He dropped the bag of fertilizer he was holding and began walking up to Raekwon's car with an awkward look on his face, as if he had no idea what was going on.

Raekwon was coldhearted when it came to handling a scandalous dopefiend. He and the homies had knocked plenty of dopefiends out for trying to get over. So, it wouldn't hurt to put hands on this fool if he chose to get fly at the mouth.

He didn't walk all the way up to the car door. He looked like he was kind of scared, as if he feared the repercussions, and Raekwon could see it in his eyes.

He always pretended as if he couldn't speak good English, but he couldn't fool Raekwon. There were plenty of occasions where he asked for credit on some dope and didn't stumble on one word, so Raekwon knew he understood what he was saying.

"You betta not go to court on my homeboy for that punk-ass bullshit you pulled," Raekwon told him.

"I not go to court. I no press any charges," he responded, fearing Raekwon would hurt him. His hands were in position, preparing to block any assault from Raekwon.

"I don't give a fuck who pressed the charges. You just betta not be there at his court date."

He said, "Okay."

Without another word, Raekwon pulled off. He would've loved to peel off to make even more of a statement. However, in that car, there was no guarantee it would make it to the next location, let alone peel out.

He looked at Carlos as they approached the stop sign, and they both burst out laughing until they damn near pissed on themselves. After the moment of amusement was over, Raekwon asked Carlos where they should go, and he suggested they go to the park they usually went to and where several others hung out.

Raekwon decided to stop by the corner store to grab something to drink since he had used the soda he had taken from RoRo's as a chaser for the Hennessy.

They pulled up to The Market, where it was popping. It wasn't a surprise because it was a normal hangout that people would usually go to. Damn near everybody would go there to stand outside of their cars drinking, smoking, and blasting their stereo systems like it was a club letting out.

The Arabs who owned the store didn't seem to mind, so neither did everybody else. The only time anyone would care about the obnoxious crowd was when the police would show up. Everyone would scatter in different directions hoping the police wouldn't follow them and pull them over.

Raekwon hopped out of the car and tried to hurry in the store to grab the drinks before the police came as usual. When he returned to the car, Carlos was across the parking lot leaning in some broad's car. Raekwon yelled for him to hurry up, and to his surprise, here comes the police to break up the festivities. The Arabs began flagging everyone off as if they cared about them being there in the first place. They would always do that when the police came. If you asked him, Raekwon would think they were the ones calling the police but didn't want them to know that.

Carlos hurried back to the car and hopped in because they didn't want to be the last of the cars to leave. After he got in, they pulled off and tried to blend in with the rest of the crowd. One of the patrol cars began coming their way, though. Raekwon made the first left, something he was never supposed to do, but at the moment, he was distorted.

Raekwon sat up stiff with both hands on the steering wheel like an old-ass nigga with arthritis, trying not to be targeted. He wasn't as uneasy as he usually got because he didn't have any dope on him.

Still, there they came right behind them, watching every move that was made. He knew they were hit when they turned with them. He got to a stop sign and made another left. As soon as Raekwon turned, they hit the lights.

"Damn!" he and Carlos shouted in disgust.

When he pulled over, they pulled over behind them immediately and with no remorse. The cop who was driving got out of the car clutching his pistol, and the cop in the passenger seat hopped out on the same bullshit as the driver.

Raekwon considered jumping out and running, but since he had gotten rid of the rest of his dope earlier that day, he didn't trip. He decided to go ahead and accept a ticket for having no license and insurance. He had his temporary tag altered, so he doubted they paid it any attention.

Once the officers approached both sides of Raekwon's car, they told them to step out. They automatically knew who they were from previous encounters.

They slapped the cuffed on Raekwon and put him in the back of the police car. When he asked them why he was being arrested, they responded by telling him that he was going to jail for the intimidation of a witness.

Raekwon told Carlos to get his car keys, but the police said they were towing the car and that the keys would be stored with the rest of his personal property at the jail. As the officer who was driving pulled off while rolling up the windows, Raekwon yelled out for Carlos to let his mother know what had happened.

CHAPTER 3

R aekwon lay in his cell on twenty-three hour lockdown. He had been in juvenile hall for two days and his patience was growing short. He was thinking about his mom, and hoping she wasn't trying to teach him a lesson by leaving him locked up.

***

Roxanne had a lot to put up with by dealing with Raekwon and his older brother Tip. She had already been through a whole lot of bullshit in her life while growing up, and now she was cursed with Raekwon, a hardheaded son that couldn't resist the street life.

Having grown up in the south, Roxanne's feet were rougher than a mechanic's hands because she had run around with no shoes on all through her early childhood years. At one point in her life, she and her siblings lived in a shack in the middle of nowhere by themselves. She told Raekwon that they had to chew on ice cubes for water and shoot birds out of the sky with slingshots just to eat. She said they never knew where they would get their next meal from, but God always made a way.

Roxanne used to be a dopefiend when she was in her mid-twenties. Raekwon still remembered the time when she had him in the backseat of the car while she rode around in the five points looking for a hit of dope. The five points was a well-known area for drugs and violence. He was about five years old at the time, but knew exactly what was going on.

She parked on the side of an abandoned building and waited. Soon after, a cab pulled up and a short, dark-skinned man with an afro got out of the backseat and walked over to the car. After the strange man handed his mother two small rocks, she put one of the rocks in her mouth and said, "Let me make sure this shit makes my tongue numb 'cause I ain't tryin' to pay for no bad dope." A few seconds later, she handed him the piece that was in her hand and said, "This stuff ain't no damn good."

The man gave her a threatening look. "I ain't got no time for these damn games. Give me the rest of my shit so I can go."

Raekwon guessed she had bitten some of the dope off, because when she took it out of her mouth and handed it to him, he stared at her with fuel in his eyes.

The man grabbed Roxanne by the throat and demanded, "Give me my muthafuckin' dope fo' I kill yo' ass."

"Alright! Alright!" she yelled, choking slightly.

Once she took the small piece of rock from underneath her tongue and handed it to him, the man walked back towards the car while suspiciously looking in all directions.

That type of stuff used to scare Raekwon to death. He guessed nobody thought you could comprehend those types of things when you're so young.

Roxanne started to change her life sometime after her cousin G-Dub got murdered on 34th Street, and she had been the backbone of the family ever since.

A heavyset white man with thick eyebrows and glasses approached the door and unlocked it. When the door swung open, he called Raekwon by his last name and said, "Pack your shit and let's go!"

He instantly jumped up, trying to hold back the smile of relief that forced its way onto his face. He let out a deep sigh of alleviation and slipped on his state-issued canvas shoes. Then he gathered his property slip along with the bed sheets and other things that had been issued upon his arrival there.

When he got to the receiving and discharge area, his mother stood on the other side of the desk. She had on a blouse with a green t-shirt underneath it, a pair of faded purple sweatpants, some black slip-on shoes with no socks, and an old stocking on her head with holes in it. She didn't care what people thought about her. She would just get up and go when something important came up. Raekwon used to get embarrassed by these public appearances when he was younger, but grew to love it because he realized how real she was.

She lowered her eyes until they looked like slits to let him know she had some words for him when they left the jail.

As they drove off, Roxanne looked at him and sighed with disappointment. "Boy, you just don't learn, do you?" She shook her head as if she was disgusted with him. "Now what you done did this time?"

At first, he was glad she had gotten him out, but now, he wished she would stop and drop him off right where they were. Raekwon hated when she hammered him about shit he already knew.

He told her that he didn't threaten that man and that he just asked him some questions. Raekwon didn't know what it was, but he could never tell his mother the whole truth about anything he got himself into.

"How you gonna sit there and lie to me, boy?" She paused, and when he gave no response, she said, "You hear me talkin' to you?"

By that time, his lips were poked all the way out and he was staring out of the window. She told him not to call her if he got into any more trouble, and she meant it.

From the time they got on the highway, all the way until they got to town, they both remained silent, lost in their own thoughts as the wind blew the noisy sounds of life's surroundings outside of the car.

When they got to the house, they got out of the car without speaking a word to each other. Raekwon went into the house and headed straight for his room in the basement. He closed his door and immediately went to the spot where he kept his money.

He still had two hundred and something odd dollars on him, but he wanted to grab a couple extra dollars to make sure he wouldn't come up short when he tried to go and get his car out of the impound. He had nine hundred dollars in his stash spot, so he took fifty dollars out and stashed the rest back in his closet.

Raekwon called Carlos to let him know he was out of jail and needed him to come and take him to get his car. Carlos told him that he would check with his dad to see if he could use the car and then he would call him right back.

After hanging up the phone, Raekwon hopped in the

shower. It felt good to get the infested scent of jail off of him.

By the time Carlos called him back, Raekwon was already out of the shower and putting his clothes on. He told Raekwon it was cool for him to use the car, so he was on his way to pick him up.

Raekwon grabbed his car title and ID and stuffed the money in his pocket, which was a couple of rusty one dollar bills over three hundred of the dope money he had been trying to save up.

Carlos pulled up blowing the horn for him to hurry up. As they were pulling off, Raekwon saw his mother looking out of the living room window shaking her head in disappointment, and he could see it written all over her face.

They got to the car impound at around one o'clock and didn't get to the front of the line until almost an hour had passed because the line was so long. When Raekwon did get to the front, they told him that he couldn't get the car out because he wasn't old enough. Raekwon was so damn angry he almost cussed out the fat, white broad behind the desk. However, he held his tongue because he had to come back sooner or later and didn't want any kind of problems.

They got back in Carlos' father's car and drove to the nearest payphone so Raekwon could call Mike, the dopefiend that had sold him the car. Mike was a pretty cool dude. He was married to Kel's aunt, so Raekwon knew him even before he started selling him dope.

He explained to Mike what had happened and told him that the lady said the previous owner could get the car out for him. Mike agreed to come because he knew there was something in it for him. He rarely did things for others from the heart because he had an addiction to feed, and he was going to feed it by any means necessary.

When Raekwon hung up the phone, he and Carlos went back to the impound to wait for Mike to show up.

Carlos said, "You know me and Kel went and fucked them broads that I had hooked up the other day."

"Oh yeah?" Raekwon responded in a tone that gave him the indication that he wanted to hear more.

"Man, them bitches was some freaks, homie," Carlos continued. "That nigga Kel is a straight fool. He was drunk as a muthafucka, all up in the bitch's refrigerator spittin' loogies on they leftover food. He pissed all on the back of they toilet and in they bathtub."

Raekwon let out a light laugh. "That nigga's crazy than a muthafucka for that."

"Yeah, you know him. He got the bitch's dog high. That muthafucka started chasing its tail and barking at its shadow. That dog was lovin' that Old E that he put in his dog bowl, too."

"Damn, that nigga was terrorizing that hoe silently, huh?" Raekwon asked. "What she do to make him do all that?"

"She ain't do nothin'. The bad thing about it was she didn't even know that nigga was doin' it. He was flickin' boogers on the walls and some mo' shit."

They both shared a laugh.

"Yeah, man, I fucked the bitch that I told you I met at the 7-11," Carlos said. "She blew my balls and everything. I busted a nut in like five minutes and told the bitch I had to use the bathroom just so I had an excuse to get up. I snuck downstairs, though, and seen that nigga Kel fuckin' the other broad on the couch. That drunk-ass nigga ain't have on nothin' but some dirty-ass socks."

"What's wrong wit' that nigga, man?" Raekwon asked with a confused look on his face.

"I don't know, but I damn near fell down the stairs laughing at that nigga. The bad thing about it was the broad's mom came home early and we had to hop out the window."

Carlos had Raekwon laughing so hard that his stomach was hurting and his eyes were watering. He had a unique way of explaining things. He always exaggerated things and put a lot of action into the way he described how something went down. Carlos and Raekwon were able to relate on a lot of subjects, which is probably what got them tight.

After spending about thirty minutes talking, Raekwon noticed Mike pulling up in his wife's raggedy-ass Riviera.

Mike got out of the car, walked over to the passenger window, and said, "What's up, man?" He hesitated for a minute and looked around. "Let me get a little piece of somethin' real quick so I can wake up."

"Shit, I ain't got no work," Raekwon responded.

Mike's eyes widened, and he looked at him like he was crazy. "What you mean you ain't got nothin'?"

Raekwon didn't respond to Mike's question. Instead, he looked at Carlos and said, "Give this fool a little somethin' before I have to get out this car and put my hands on him."

Carlos handed Mike a dime piece of crack. "Here, man."

After getting his car out the impound, Raekwon hurried to the service station that was up the block so he could get some gas. He popped the trunk open to see if the case of beer was still in there and then popped open the inside paneling in the back seat to make sure his .22 revolver was still there, too. To his relief, everything was still in its place.

Raekwon followed Carlos back to town so he could return his dad's car. After he dropped the car off, he hopped in Raekwon's car with him. Raekwon told him that he needed to re-up on his dope so he was going to roll to the house and call Mace.

Mace, who was seven years older than Raekwon, was one of them mulatto niggas that got all the hoes. Raekwon met Mace when he was young and throwing rocks at people out of trees. He used to hang with Dean and Darryl that lived up the street from him. Dean and Darryl were two brothers that always had a basement full of broads and kept the street flooded with nice cars. Raekwon was fascinated by the way they had shit jumping off. He was only eleven years old around the time he really began to observe their lifestyle. By the time he was twelve years old, he was slipping through their back door with everybody else and making himself at home. He was trying to pick up game so he could grow up and do it how they were doing it.

He remembered the first time Darryl offered him a beer. He gave him a cautious, surprised look that spoke for itself.

"Don't tell yo' mom I was the nigga that got you drunk either," Darryl told him. "I don't want her down here trying to kick my ass," he joked.

Raekwon couldn't deny that those twenty-two ounces of malt liquor put him on his ass before he realized he had finished the bottle.

Another reason Raekwon liked to go over there was because the broads would flirt with him by pinching on his cheeks and telling him that he was going to be good-looking when he grew up. Little did they know, he was trying to fuck any one of them, and he didn't care how much older than him they were.

When they pulled up to his house, he grabbed the case of beer out of the trunk and took it downstairs to the deep freezer that was halfway full with some backdated, freezer burnt meat. After placing the beer in the freezer, he grabbed the phone so he could page Mace.

By the time Mace called back, he had a basement full of niggas. Three hours had passed by, and Raekwon was kind of bitter about the fact that he felt like he left him hanging. RoRo had been blowing his pager up with all kinds of dollar amounts, and that was good money being missed.

"What's up?" Mace asked when Raekwon answered the phone.

"Damn, nigga, what took you so long? I've been missin' out on a gang of bread, homie."

"My bad, lil' homie," Mace replied. "I been knocked out all damn day. I'm on my way, though. I'll be over there in about fifteen minutes."

They hung up.

Mace already knew Raekwon wanted a half ounce of dope because he put code '400' in his pager.

Raekwon waited outside for Mace to pull up. When he did, Raekwon hopped inside of Mace's minivan. Mace reached over, turned on the interior light, and handed him the sack of dope.

Raekwon looked at the sack in a peculiar manner, as if he didn't want to get it. "This shit looks kinda short," he expressed and began to hand it back to him. "What you want for this, three-fifty? Look at all the crumbs at the bottom of the sack. I can't do nothin' with that."

Mace smacked his lips and smirked while stroking his chin, as if he was considering his plea. After he thought for a minute, he said, "That was the last of my sack, but it weighs fifteen-one with the bag."

"I'm gonna lose some when I re-rock the shit, though," Raekwon explained with a convincing screech in his voice.

"Alright, I'll do it for you this time," he responded, then gave him a look as if he was saying Raekwon knew too much about the dope game to be so young.

When Raekwon went back in the basement, niggas was loud off of the liquor. He was a little tipsy, too, and wanted something to get into.

"I got these lil' broads coming over that me and Raylin was fuckin' wit' last night. They some nasty bitches. They just called from the payphone at the Market and asked for directions from there," Dre said, while twisting the top off of his beer.

Dre lived a couple of houses down from Raekwon, and Raylin lived right across the street from him. So, there was always something festive going on down the block. People would ride down their block just to see if anything was going down. They always kept the block popping, even if it was just a couple of homies standing out by their cars drinking. The police would always hit the block and drive by real slow. They were trying to observe everybody and everything that was going on.

They had been chilling for quite some time after the broads that Dre hooked up finally hit the scene. Raekwon's big brother Tip was trying to make them laugh by cracking jokes. He was a funny nigga to be around because he always had something to say. He started roasting one of the broads.

"Damn, yo' hair short," Tip said. "Is that supposed to be some kinda style or something?"

She rolled her eyes at him. When everybody started laughing, she started to look embarrassed.

Tip continued with his verbal assault. "Girl, you smell like you grabbed them clothes from the bottom of the dirty clothes basket."

The cold thing about it was that Tip was sandwiched between both of the broads on the couch. Niggas was laughing so hard that Raekwon's mother began to stomp on the floor. That was Roxanne's way of telling them that we were too loud.

When the jokes died down, the broad named Tanya, who was the center of attention, sat in silence as she rambled through her purse. Her body language conveyed her anger. After removing a small piece of paper from her purse, she stood up and began to walk towards the phone.

Dre, who was sitting next to the phone, picked it up and began to use it just out of spite.

Tanya turned back around, retraced her steps back to the couch, and said, "Niggas ain't shit."

She sat down next to her homegirl Jada, and shortly after she whispered a couple of words in Jada's ear, they got up and left.

Raekwon didn't care if they left or not because something about them just didn't click with him anyway. When he finally began to watch his situations in life play out, he started to look at things in more of a scientific way. He started to notice the patterns of his everyday experiences advancing, but everyday reminded him of a day he had experienced before, full of nothing.

He knew there had to be a bigger picture than what he was seeing. He always had a feeling that life wasn't just about selling dope, fucking broads, and roaming the earth with no sense of direction. However, the type of life he was surrounded by wasn't teaching him that. He had to learn his own way, which seemed like it was going to be the hard way.

CHAPTER 4

"Caught one in the leg and now I'm stuck; if they let me out alive, man, them niggas betta duck," spat Juan, rapping like he meant every word that came out of his mouth.

The music was knocking like an engine in an old-ass Buick. They were spitting some lyrics to a beat Raekwon had made, trying to get a song together so they could finish the album they had started a while back.

Raekwon had been into writing his own lyrics for a while by this time, and now he was good at it. He had started to make his own beats two years before because older niggas was always selling him dreams. They would tell him that they were going to take him to the studio, but when the time came to go, nobody would show up to pick him up and then the niggas wouldn't return his pages. When they did give him something to write to, it was garbage most of the time. He was into that mob music. Raekwon always listened to such artists as E-40, C-Bo, Sean T., and Chunk. He couldn't settle for anything else, and therefore, he had to try to get good at it.

"Juan, turn that shit down some!" his mother yelled. She didn't like rap, but she dealt with it as long as it wasn't too loud. They would usually be in the basement when she wasn't home, and she was gone most of the time.

He turned down the music a little bit and told Raekwon that she was getting ready to leave anyway. By now, it was time to smoke a little weed. They hated to have to get up and go outside all of the time just to get high when they were in a big-ass unfinished basement.

It smelled like piss, dirty clothes, and like there was some old-ass pickle juice stained somewhere on the floor. Juan always kept the lights dimmed down there, and they were either blue or green. Their kitchen was always filthy. It was one of those kitchens that you always had to wash a cup out first if you wanted something to drink because there weren't many dishes to work with. Their bathtub or shower didn't work. So, you can imagine how they smelled most of the time if they didn't wash up in the sink.

"Let me see a razor so I can cut this blunt open."

"Look over there on that table next to my bed," Juan told Raekwon while on his way upstairs. "I'll be right back. Let me go grab these brews out of the freezer and see if my mom is gone."

Raekwon sat down and rolled up the blunt. He was supposed to be in school, but a lot of time he didn't go because he had no interest in sitting in a classroom trying to learn things he wasn't interested in.

Hearing somebody coming down the stairs, Raekwon called Juan's name, but nobody responded. He couldn't see who it was because the living room curtain that served as a door was blocking his view.

"Hey, what's up? You doing anything?" Juan's pops asked in a whisper after pulling the curtain back and noticing Raekwon sitting there.

Juan's pop was an old-school dopefiend that hustled the blocks day in and day out. Everybody called him Mitchy Moe, and he had been in the game since heroin was popular. Raekwon fucked with Moe on the regular. He was such a good customer that he would give him damn near double of whatever he spent with him just so he would come back.

When Raekwon told him that he was working, Moe handed him sixty dollars. Raekwon reached in his pocket and pulled out his sack. He handed him a hundred dollars' worth of dope and was surprised he didn't ask for a bump more like he normally did. Raekwon asked Moe what Juan was up there doing, and he said that when he pulled up, Juan was standing outside talking to LP and Nick.

Raekwon went upstairs and through the garage, which was open. Juan's raggedy K5 Blazer was sitting in there with the hood open, and the neighborhood dopefiend mechanic, Will, was underneath the truck working on it. It seemed like every time he worked on somebody's car, it would only be mobile for no more than a month or two before it would start acting up again.

"Fuck!" Will yelled and started kicking his feet.

"What the fuck you done did now?" Raekwon asked in a sarcastic voice.

"Get this motherfucker off of me!"

Juan, LP, and Nick ran to the garage and looked under the truck. Will had just rolled from under the transmission. It seemed like every time he tried to fix somebody's car, he hurt one of his body parts. He was definitely one of the craziest white boys that Raekwon had ever met. He always rode around the neighborhood on a ten-speed, trying to get some credit from somebody most of the time.

After they knew Will was going to be cool, they walked out of the garage and stood over by LP's Impala. LP mentioned a party that Alexis and Destiny were throwing, and they all decided that they were going to go because they knew it would be cracking if they were throwing it. Alexis and Destiny got along with damn near all of the broads that they went to school with, so they knew it was going to be a cool little scene to be at. Raekwon asked Nick where they were having the party, and he told him that it was supposed to be at Destiny's big sister's apartment complex, clubhouse.

***

Upon pulling up in the parking lot of the apartments, they heard music. They parked in the front of the clubhouse and sat in the car for a while because Raekwon hadn't finished his forty ounce of beer yet. After he and LP sat in the car for about fifteen minutes talking and listening to music, they decided to go in. Juan and Nick were supposed to meet them in the parking lot, but he had a feeling they were not going to show up.

They walked up the stairs and approached the door. At the door was a chocolate woman who could not have been any older than twenty years old. She had on a tight beige skirt and a see-through white sleeveless shirt with a tan sports bra underneath it. Her hair was black and silky, and it came down to her shoulders. Her complexion was caramel, and her skin looked smooth and soft enough to put a nigga to sleep if he came in contact with it. He stared at her in a way that said exactly what he was thinking; *Damn, you look good.* Raekwon didn't bother to notice the dude standing behind her, but the dude sure did notice Raekwon. He gave him a violating smirk as if Raekwon had disrespected him in some way. He had to be at least three or four years older than everybody else that was at the party, and Raekwon could tell the nigga was a gangbanger by the way he was dressed. He chalked the look off as a small thing that he shouldn't worry about, but only after he returned a similar look back in his direction.

With the music banging, Raekwon and LP made their way through the crowd to go and see who the DJ was so they could try to get him to play one of the songs Raekwon had recorded in the studio. He got over to the DJ booth, but didn't know the DJ personally. Still, he had seen him around before. He approached him, lifted the left side of the headphones off the DJ's ear, and leaned toward him. The DJ was sweating like he had just got through running from the district five police, so Raekwon made sure not to get too close.

"What's up, lil' homie?"

"Aye doe, check this out. I was trying to see if you'll play one of my songs. The shit ain't no garbage either," Raekwon told him.

"You got it on vinyl?" the DJ asked, catching him off guard.

"Naw." Raekwon's smile was replaced with a confused look.

It seemed like getting a DJ to play his music at a party was one of the hardest things to do. He never wanted to understand that vinyl shit for nothing in the world. He didn't even know who to ask if he did want his recordings on vinyl. All he knew was he had a tape in his pocket with some good music on it that he wanted somebody to play at a party.

The beer he drank before going inside started getting him in that superfly mode, and he began to glide through the room like he owned the place. He walked over to the corner where a couple of his homies were shooting dice. Raekwon was sweating like an obese person trying to finish the rest of a hamburger.

"Bet he six-eight!" he yelled when LP caught eight as a point.

"Bet that money!" Ken tossed two, twenty-dollar bills next to Raekwon's foot and then kneeled down on his right knee with his right hand on the floor to hold his balance and his left forearm resting on his left knee.

Ken was a hustler and one of the luckiest niggas to lay fingers on a pair of dice. He practically lived at the crap house. Raekwon had seen dudes literally ball-up their fists and cut their eyes at Ken before. He probably would have been dead if he wasn't the type of person that would break up the dice game and give niggas back half of what he hit for.

"Bet then, nigga!" Raekwon reached in his pocket, peeled off two twenties, and threw them on top of his.

"E-I-G-H-T!" LP yelled and rolled the dice out of his hand, hitting a six.

Raekwon picked up two twenties and looked at Ken. "Bet back."

"Bet." Ken threw two more twenties on top of the two that were there.

LP shook the dice and looked at the dude that was fading him. "When you see four topless bitches," he paused and released the dice, "how many nipples do you see?"

There was silence.

"Eight, nigga! Point seen! Money gone!" LP had the world in his hands by the way he emphasized his comment.

They both picked up that time. Raekwon got up and told LP that he was about to go and see who was downstairs. It was off the hook when he did. There was a steam room downstairs, and niggas was in there hot-boxing. They were rolling weed and getting at broads.

When Raekwon went into the bathroom to take a piss, it didn't seem like the place where you would go to use the bathroom the way niggas were in there hanging out, drinking, and smoking. The awkward thing about it was there were broads in the men's restroom. It didn't bother him, though. So, he didn't ask any questions. The bathroom was hella foggy due to all of the weed, cigarette, and Black & Mild smoke.

Raekwon could barely breathe, so he decided he was going to go holler at a couple of broads and chill with the thugs on the wall. He stepped out of the bathroom and began to make his way through the hot, crowded hallway. While walking with his head turned to the left, he accidentally bumped into somebody and stepped on their shoe.

"My bad, homie." Raekwon put his hands up to make sure the dude didn't fall.

"Damn, nigga. Watch where the fuck you goin'," the guy said, trying to pop real fly after he saw who he was.

It was the same nigga that gave him the crazy-ass smirk while he was looking at the broad when he first stepped inside the party. He could tell the dude was trying to turn a small situation into a big problem. Raekwon figured the broad that he was checking-out earlier was his girl, and that he was causing the issue now because of their run-in earlier over that stank-ass bitch.

"You fucked up my shoes, cuz," he started, acting like he was one of the hardest niggas alive.

"Whatever, nigga," Raekwon replied.

"What you tryin' to say?"

One of his homeboys came over and said, "What, is this lil' nigga tryin' to see some problems or somethin'?"

"Naw, I don't think this lil' muthafucka tryin' to see me."

They had size on Raekwon, but at that point, none of that mattered because if any one of them were to hit him, it was going to be on.

LP walked up, looked at the situation for like ten seconds, then just walked off and back up the stairs. He looked like he was mad about something, but he didn't say anything.

Where in the fuck is that nigga going? Raekwon asked himself. *How come he didn't try to help me? What if these niggas try to jump me or somethin'?*

"Why you step on my shit, cuz?" He just wouldn't let it go, and at the same time, he was waiting for Raekwon to make the first move.

Raekwon could tell the dude didn't just want to swing on a young buck first over something he knew was some bullshit.

"Whatever, man. Y'all niggas is trippin'." At that point, Raekwon began to get mad and they noticed.

"What you trying to do then, lil' nigga?"

LP walked back down the stairs and over to where Raekwon was standing.

"Y'all niggas is still trippin'?" LP asked with a serious look on his face.

Everybody who was standing around looked at LP and noticed his shirt lifted up. Raekwon thought they were about to get down with those niggas until he noticed LP pulling a .375 magnum from out of his pants. Raekwon stood next to him, mugging them like he was ready for whatever.

They must have thought they were some kind of superheroes that couldn't be touched. The one who started the whole misunderstanding in the first place had the idea that he was dealing with a young punk. Raekwon could see right through the tough-man act that he was portraying. He really didn't expect the homeboy to go out to the car and come back with a pistol.

"What you gonna do, lil' nigga?" He jumped out there with his mouth by saying a couple more words, which was too many.

Boom! LP blasted him in the shoulder. All Raekwon could hear was a loud echo and a ringing noise in his ear. When he snapped back to reality, he realized LP had just shot him. Everyone was yelling, screaming, and running for their lives like an earthquake had just hit. People were diving on the floor and tripping over each other everywhere he looked.

Raekwon shut down and began to have tunnel vision. All he noticed was LP walking up the stairs with the gun still in his hand. He followed behind him. When they got upstairs, LP's cousin Vanessa ran over to him. He didn't stop, though. He was walking towards the front door like a madman. Raekwon followed closely behind. He noticed people running and ducking out of sight as if they didn't trust them. These were the same people that came around all the time when a nigga had some weed to smoke and some liquor to drink.

"What happened, LP? What happened?" Vanessa asked, out of breath from running. "Are you okay? Who was it that got shot?"

The three of them headed towards LP's car once they were outside in the parking lot. By then, Vanessa had started questioning both of them. Raekwon told her that he didn't know what had happened and for her to go back inside of the clubhouse.

BOOM! BOOM! BOOM! The niggas came running through the parking lot toward them, blasting with no remorse.

Raekwon tried to open the front passenger door on LP's car while crouching down, but it was locked. LP was kneeling down on the ground by the front tire. Everything was happening so fast that Raekwon didn't really know how to react since he didn't have his gun with him to shoot back. He tried to slide underneath the car, but he couldn't fit up under it. He didn't want to go out like that. All he could hear were gunshots, but he didn't know what direction they were shooting from.

Raekwon took a life-threatening chance and got up off the ground yelling for LP and Vanessa to come on. He ran back towards the clubhouse as more shots rang out. He heard a bullet whisper in his ear while he rushed up the stairs and into the clubhouse. He yanked the door open and dived onto the floor. Raekwon then hopped to his feet and began pushing people out of the way so he could find somewhere to chill for a minute until the scene was clear.

He ran to and opened the first closet door he saw. It was a closet packed full of females who had some of the scariest looks on their faces that he'd ever seen. He could tell just by those looks that they thought he was going to do something to them. Raekwon stepped into the closet and tried to shut it behind him, but two of the broads pushed it back open and ran out. When they ran up out of there, the rest of the broads followed right behind them.

Already mad, he threw the closet door open as hard as he could and yelled out, "Fuck all y'all punk-ass bitches."

Raekwon went back outside with a fuck-it attitude. He was so mad and distorted that he didn't care what happened at that point. Kayla, who was standing outside, walked up to him and asked if he was okay. He told her that he was cool and asked if she had seen where LP went. She told him that she didn't know where LP went, but that she did know Vanessa got shot in the shoulder and the ass. Raekwon got quiet and started doing the math. He realized those two bullets that Vanessa took were intended for him and LP.

LP's car was still parked in the same place, but he was nowhere to be found. When Raekwon began to walk off, Kayla asked him where he was going. He told her that he was going to walk home. Just then, Lil' Rob, who Raekwon sometimes kicked it with, came running across the parking lot to make sure he was cool. Lil' Rob decided he was going to walk with them, and after a couple of blocks, he turned off. Kayla ended up walking with Raekwon all the way home. He went to her grandma's house with her to use the phone so he could call LP to make sure he was okay. Raekwon called his house, and LP's mother answered.

"Hello, Ms. Palmer. Can I speak to Lonnie?"

"He hasn't come home yet. I thought he was with you?"

Raekwon improvised. Lying through his teeth, he said,

"Yeah, that was earlier, but I had to go help my mom do something and he left."

He thought she was going to ask him some particular questions after that to try to catch him in a lie. She would usually probe for an answer, but she left it at that. They said their goodbyes and hung up.

Next, Raekwon called over to LP's girl's house.

"Hey, girl, what's up? Have you seen LP?" he asked as soon as she picked up.

"Yeah, here he goes. Hold up."

Raekwon was relieved to know that he was okay.

"Hello." You could hear it in LP's voice that he was a little paranoid as to who was going to respond on the other end of the phone.

"What's up, nigga? Is you okay?" Raekwon asked in a concerned voice.

"Yeah, I was trippin' on that shit, too, my nigga."

Raekwon paused. "Is she okay?"

LP sighed. "I don't know because ain't nobody called to let me know nothing yet."

There was a few seconds of silence before Raekwon asked, "Where did you go? Nigga, I was lookin' all over for you."

"One of Vanessa's friends dropped me off before she took Vanessa to the hospital. Vanessa wanted me to go with them, but I told her that I couldn't go because the people at the hospital was gonna call the police. I didn't want to end up getting identified and go to jail."

Raekwon asked, "When are you going to get your car?"

"By tomorrow things should be cooled down. I'll go and get it then," LP replied, and then they hung up.

Kayla walked up to Raekwon with a concerned look. "Is he alright?"

"Yeah, he's alright, just a little paranoid."

"He should be," she said, like she was the one paranoid.

Raekwon got up. "I'm going home. I'll catch up with you later," he told her and then left.

Kayla was six months pregnant at the time by some nigga that she didn't get along with anymore. She didn't have any business being at that party anyway.

Raekwon and Kayla ended up getting real tight after that. They were on some brother-and-sister type of bonding and didn't compromise it for anything. She used to write lyrics, too. Soon, Raekwon introduced her to the dope game.

One day, Raekwon and Kayla were walking down the street on their way to a studio that a dopefiend had in his basement, when Raekwon got flagged down by one of his regular customers. When the dopefiend asked for twenty dollars' worth of dope, Raekwon gave it to Kayla to give to him.

"That's all I have to do is give it to him and get the money?" she asked with a curious look on her face.

"Yeah, girl, go ahead. You can keep the money, too." Raekwon gave her a look of assurance and nodded his head.

He could tell she was desperate for some kind of hustle. She was pregnant at fourteen years old and didn't have a job, but she needed to support her and her baby.

***

Life was rough. Raekwon started taking his gun to school with him because he was paranoid. Haunted with visions of those niggas retaliating and murdering him and LP, he took no chances at being caught without a strap again. He couldn't just

55

hop out of the life he was living, even though he sometimes felt like he wanted to. This wasn't a game he was playing. It was the game he was living.

Raekwon started cutting certain people off. He realized he couldn't be messing around with just anyone out there in the streets. It wasn't the streets that were trying to kill him; it was the niggas in the streets that wanted him dead. It was time to do some serious thinking, and he couldn't do that with his head blown off.

THE SEAL OF RUIN

CHAPTER 5

Raekwon was desperate. He sat in his basement alone, writing down the phone numbers inside of tape covers of rap artists that were from Denver. He was eager to get somebody to hear his music. He had been recording a lot of songs in the last couple of months and those in the streets that were hearing his shit were telling him it was banging. He had been going over to Primo's, the dopefiend that Kayla had introduced him to. Raekwon gave him dope in exchange for him sitting in his basement and making beats on his ASR 10. Raekwon was putting in a lot of work, but it seemed like it wasn't paying off. His stepdad bought him a Korg O1/W synthesizer, and he learned how to make beats on it after a couple of months. He was all the way in the game now. His name was getting out there, and niggas wanted to be a part of what he was doing.

He sat on the edge of his bed in a deep daydream and started thinking about everything he was going through. Everything he had been through triggered the fact that nothing was working in his favor. This was the turning point in his life, and he was beginning to realize that. Things weren't going to be as easy as it used to be. His mother stopped buying him shoes and clothes. She stopped giving him loose change, and she didn't even bother pressuring him about getting a job. Raekwon thought she had an idea that he was hustling, and at this point, he didn't really have a choice but to hustle.

Growing up in poverty was mirrored in every tear that escaped from his eyes. Opening up the icebox to a spoiled carton of milk or not having enough milk in it to make a bowl of cereal, so he would have to add some water with it. Nothing but an open package of bologna with dried-up edges around all the pieces, a block of government cheese sitting on the second shelf in a cardboard container, and a generic white box on top of the refrigerator labeled 'Saltines'.

Raekwon started acting out a lot when he was twelve. Sometime after he got dropped on his head, split his shit to the white meat, and had to get rushed to the hospital to get stitches, he became very disobedient. Roxanne would actually kick him out of the house at twelve and thirteen years of age for either not wanting to go to church, school, or for not doing things she wanted him to do around the house.

"Get out!" she would scream, and she meant every word. He could see it in her eyes that she really meant it. She even changed all of the locks on him at one point because he would sneak back in the house when she wasn't home.

He used to sleep in abandoned vans, clubhouses that he and the homies built, or would wear out his welcome at his friends' houses until he had nowhere else to go.

He began to shake his head, remembering when he was twelve and went to a local rap-off with Kel. His two female cousins, who were about the same age as him, were also there. They were pretty tight on the mic to be some young females.

They all sat at a table by the stage watching people perform. All of a sudden, Kel's big cousin Roscoe, who was the host, announced there was going to be a freestyle contest. Raekwon had no intentions of getting involved in it, but Courtney and Leslie pointed their fingers and got all of the attention on him to go up there. He was the youngest one in the contest and ended up winning.

Raekwon didn't get home until about two in the morning and was drunk off of some Mad Dog. Roxanne had been sitting on the couch in the living room waiting for him to show up, and she had a vicious look on her face until she saw the trophy in his hand. She was angry at him, but at the same time, she was proud of him for winning at something she knew he liked to do. Music was what he wanted to do, and there was nothing that could change his mind.

"Hey, nigga," Kel said, while walking into the room and interrupting Raekwon's reminiscing.

"What's up?" Raekwon responded, then looked at him for a second before asking, "How did you get in?"

"The back door was unlocked."

"Oh yeah. Where you coming from?"

"I just came from smokin' a joint wit' my pops at the house."

"You ain't got no more?"

"Nope, but I know where to get some. You got ten on it?"

"Hell yeah." Raekwon needed to smoke a little bit of weed after all the stressing he had been doing.

"Take me around there by Ty's house."

"Dat nigga selling weed now?" Raekwon asked in a high-pitched voice.

"Naw, his mom sells that shit. Where yo' car at?" He looked at Raekwon and anticipated an answer.

"I parked it around the corner."

Raekwon started parking his car around the corner because his stepdad began tripping with him about the oil that was leaking from it.

He got up off of the bed and grabbed his keys off of the dresser. When he walked around the corner to get in his car, it was gone.

"What the fuck!" He looked around confused.

"What happened?" Kel chuckled. "Somebody stole yo' shit or somethin'?"

"I think my shit got towed," Raekwon replied with anger. "The bitch that lives in the corner house right there is always watching me park my shit on the side of her muthafuckin' house."

Raekwon was so mad that he went to knock on the lady's door to ask her if she called for his car to get towed. Nobody answered, so they went back to Raekwon's house and back into the basement, which they referred to as The Dungeon.

When Raekwon called the car impound, he was told they hadn't received it there. He knew his car wouldn't last long whether it was because it broke down, was impounded by the police, was stolen by a local thug, or was totaled as a result of him driving around town like a speed demon.

He gave up trying to figure out what had happened to it. Instead, he called Carlos to come and take him and Kel to get the weed and something to eat. Carlos said he would be there in twenty minutes. So, Raekwon and Kel decided to go outside to wait. Noticing Dre and Raylin sitting outside of Dre's house in the driveway, they walked down the street to where they were drinking some brews.

"Where yo' car at?" Dre asked, looking at him with a curious expression on his face.

"I think the police stole my shit from around there where I been parkin' it."

"Damn, that's fucked up," Raylin commented with his mouth wide open in disbelief.

"What y'all niggas 'bout to do?" Raekwon asked that question like he was looking for something to get into.

"Shit, we waitin' fo' these bitches to come through." Dre had a smirk on his face like he was up to something sneaky.

"Who y'all got comin' over?"

"Nikki and her little punk-ass partners."

"Damn, I've been wantin' to fuck that bitch since seventh grade," Raekwon said.

"Me, too." Dre agreed the broad was ready to get dicked down properly.

When Carlos pulled up, Raekwon and Kel hopped in the car.

"Where y'all niggas 'bout to go?" Raylin asked.

"We're going to get something to eat, and then we're probably going to get some weed," Raekwon replied as they pulled off.

They went to get the weed from Ty's mother first because Raekwon pressed the issue. Kel was hungry already because he was coming down from the weed he had smoked with his pops.

"Look," Raekwon said, "if we get the weed first and smoke

on our way to get something to eat, we'll have the munchies by the time we get there. Y'all niggas is supposed to already know that shit. Oh yeah, I forgot. Kel's already blowed."

"Shit, nigga, that was my pop's shit. He knows I smoke now, so I can't just pinch from his sack like I used to when we first started smoking. Nigga, you betta be glad I'm pitching in on this sack that we 'bout to go get right now."

Carlos interrupted. "Y'all fools is always arguing over some dumb-ass shit."

They pulled up to Ty's house, where he was sitting on the porch with his newborn Rottweiler puppies trying to sell one to a dude that lived up the block from him named Squachy that everybody called Ugly Cuz Capone. That was his gang name. Squachy didn't get along with Kel. So, as soon as they pulled up, Raekwon knew it was about to be a fight.

Somebody broke into Squachy's house a while back and stole his stereo, six hundred dollars in cash, a quarter pound of weed, and a pistol. He said some broad that he use to fuck overheard Kel talking about how he came up on some money and weed from a lick that he hit. Raekwon didn't know if Kel did it or not because he never spoke on it around him.

Ty and Squachy stopped what they were doing when they saw the car pulling up.

Kel said, "Aw, this bitch-ass nigga is 'bout to be on this bullshit about what some punk-ass bitch told him."

Carlos parked the car and turned around to look at Kel. "Oh yeah, that fool did say somebody told him that you was the one that broke into his house."

They gave Carlos their money for the weed before all of them got out of the car and walked up to the porch. Carlos went in the house, while Raekwon and Kel walked up to Ty to see the puppies.

Kel picked up one of the puppies and admired what he saw. "How much you want for this little muthafucka, Ty?"

Ty looked at Kel and said, "Shit, just give a nigga one-fifty if you really trying to get it."

Squachy stared at Kel with fire in his eyes. He was burning a hole in the back of Kel's shirt from looking so hard. Kel must have felt a bad vibe, because he turned around after he put the puppy down and noticed how vicious Squachy was looking at him.

"Nigga, what the fuck you looking at me like that for?"

"Fuck you, nigga."

"Fuck you," Kel responded. "What's up then, bitch-ass nigga? What you tryin' to do?"

They both stepped off the porch and into the grass. As Squachy started to reach in his pocket, Kel charged at him and tackled him. They wrestled around in the dirt-patched grass trying to get an advantage over one another. Kel managed to put him in a headlock and started hitting him in the side of his face. Nosy neighbors started to come outside to watch.

"Let me up!" Squachy tried to convince Kel that he was done. "You got me! You got me!"

"Naw, nigga, I know you got a knife in your pocket. You must think I'm stupid." He paused to take a breath. "I ought to kick you in yo' muthafuckin' face."

Ty's mother came out of the front door with a tall can of Old English in her hand, wearing some house shoes and a nightgown. "Y'all better get the fuck away from my house with that bullshit!" She sat her beer on the brick window ledge. "Ty,

65

get these trifling niggas the fuck away from here. You know that old-ass bitch across the street is always callin' the police on us."

Ty's mother didn't really trip off of much, but she couldn't stand for niggas to make her house a hotspot in the eyes of the neighbors and the police. Raekwon had known Ty since he was about seven years old because they used to hang out together in elementary. His grandmother was the one that tripped. When she tripped, she tripped hard. When they were little, she used to whoop Raekwon's ass, too, if he was over there when Ty got into some trouble. If she had been at the house, she probably would've chased Squachy and Kel off the block with her shotgun.

Ty's mother stood in between Kel and Squachy, who were both breathing like they were about to pass out. They had dirt stained in their clothes and caked-up on the bottoms of their shoes. Squachy's eyes were swollen, and Kel had a bloody nose that he was wiping with his shirt.

Carlos and Ty had looks on their faces that displayed they thought the two of their friends were just acting plain stupid. Raekwon and Carlos went and hopped in the car, while Kel walked into the house so he could go get some tissue. Squachy walked down the street, looking back at Kel while biting his bottom lip.

Before getting out of earshot, Squachy shouted to Kel, "Yeah, punk-ass nigga, I'ma catch up wit' you! Watch!"

"Nigga, fuck you!" Kel yelled at the top of his lungs before going inside.

As Raekwon pulled up to Burger King to order some food, he noticed a light grey car sitting across the parking lot of the shopping center. After they got their food, he told Carlos to drive over to the car so he could see if it was for sale.

They pulled up next to it and Raekwon got out. It was a 1977 Chevy Impala. It had a "For Sale" sign in the front window with an asking price of five hundred dollars.

He wrote down the number and then told Carlos to take him by the house. Once there, he called the lady and ended up talking her down to four hundred and fifty dollars. An hour later, he was rolling again.

***

It was getting late. Raekwon had been driving around all night chilling with the homies and drinking like a fish. He decided to go home and call up DG to bring him a quarter-ounce of dope. He started getting his dope from DG after Mace gave him some bad shit that all of the dopefiends complained about.

DG was older, like twenty-four or so, and also a rapper. His music wasn't all that good, but he wanted to try to put his own recordings out under his label. Since he lived across town, it would usually take an hour or so for him to get to The Maze

Raekwon unraveled the sack and placed the dope on the round glass dinner table sitting in the basement. He then went into his room to grab a razor and some sandwich bags. He chopped up the quarter-ounce into nice-sized twenty rocks so his customers wouldn't complain. He made five piles of one hundred dollars' worth of dope and even had some crumbs left. So, he added them to the crumb sack that he already had stashed in the room.

The phone rang, and it was Camilla.

He had been trying to holler at Camilla for a while, but she always had a man. She was a cheerleader, short and thick. She had a caramel complexion, sported a Halle Berry haircut, and had one of the most beautiful smiles he had ever seen. Her high cheekbones and petite waistline only added to her heart-stopping features. It was something about her that gave him the chills...in a good way. It might have been her fat ass and the fact that their birthdays were in the same month.

"Hey, boy, what you doing?" she asked.

Raekwon got out of the chair and lay on his back on the floor. "I ain't doing nothing but relaxing, trying to find something to watch on TV."

He was lying, but she didn't know, so it didn't matter.

"Did you watch the news?" The level of her voice dropped to a tone of disappointment.

"News? Why? What happened?"

"You know that girl named Renee that lives around the corner from you?"

"Uh, Brandon's sister Renee?"

"Yeah, that's her. Well, she was pregnant and nobody knew about it. I guess she didn't want her mom to find out that she was pregnant. So, she had the baby and threw it over the fence."

"That shit is crazy. I was wondering why I saw a lot of police riding around the neighborhood all day."

They started talking about all kinds of things. Raekwon would always try to keep her on the phone for a while so he could get in real good with her. There was something she liked about him, but she always played the hard-to-get role. He didn't know how long they'd talked because he ended up falling asleep on the phone.

Early the next morning, Roxanne came down the stairs to try to wake him up for school. She put her foot on his waist and shook him.

"Alright, alright," Raekwon said groggily. "I'm getting ready to get up in a minute."

"Why is you laying here sleep on this floor?" She sniffed and looked around. "Boy, is you drunk or somethin'?"

He had forgotten about the dope he had cut up and left out on the table. She walked towards the table with her neck stuck out as if she was taking precautions about something she had seen. "What in the hell is this over here on this table, some cut-up soap?"

Raekwon hopped up instantly. He knew he had slipped. His mother had never seen him with any dope before. She had never even seen him making a sale before or even engaging in any activities that looked as if he had anything to do with drugs.

She picked up a crumb and put it in her mouth, while Raekwon scraped the dope off of the table and into his hand. She began to spit like she ate some spoiled black-eyed peas.

"Where in the hell did you get that shit from?"

She grabbed Raekwon's wrist and tried to get him to let go of the dope. He clutched his hand as tight as he could.

"Oh, you think you strong, huh?" she rhetorically asked, then started hitting his wrist with her closed fist. She stopped. "Where did you get it from?"

"I got it from this dude around the corner?" He was lying through his front teeth, but he knew to never tell on anyone about anything.

"What's his name?"

"I don't know." He smacked his lips and poked his mouth

out.

"I don't know what you poking yo' mouth out for 'cause you done messed up big time." She mimicked him with sarcasm and said, "Take it back where you got it from."

"How am I gonna just take it back?"

"I don't know and I don't care, but get it out of my house right now," she demanded.

She was extremely upset and Raekwon couldn't blame her. He knew it was affecting her heart real deep because of how drugs almost destroyed her life. Luckily, she made it out of her situation.

Everywhere he went, she followed him. She wanted him to get up out of the house that very moment with no delay.

After dressing, Raekwon walked around the corner to Big Vic's house. Big Vic's mother left the house every morning before seven o'clock. The front door was already open, so he just walked in. Vic and Raylin were sitting in the living room. Raylin was rolling up some weed, while Vic was flicking through the channels on the TV.

"What's up, my niggas?" Raekwon said.

They could tell by the expression on his face that he had something on his mind that was bothering him.

"What the fuck is wrong with you?" Vic asked.

Vic was tall with retarded strength. He was usually always in a joking mood and knew how to make fun of almost everything. He was always getting kicked out of school for beating somebody's ass or cussing out one of his teachers or a female classmate.

Vic's mother grew weed in the backyard, and she also smoked it. She was a vet at it, but as soon as something happened in the neighborhood, she would pose as if she was one of the most civilized people in the city. Everybody called her Ms. G. She was real nice, but she couldn't stand for them to be at her house if they were supposed to be at school.

Vic's brother's name was Isaac. He was a crazy-ass nigga. He used to have a short temper, especially when it came to fixing on his cars. If things didn't go his way, he would punch a hole in the wall and cuss everybody out. Then hop in one of his cars and peel off. Raekwon considered him to be one of his big homies. He used to always push Raekwon to keep doing his music. He wrote lyrics sometimes, too, and he loved to listen to Tupac's *Above the Law*. Couldn't nobody tell him shit when he popped that in the deck. He would get loud and crazy off of that music, especially when he was drunk. Ms. G would always yell down in the basement for him to turn it down, and he would yell back for her to chillout.

Raekwon remembered a time when he was over at Vic and Isaac's house, and Isaac walked to his car that was parked on the curb in front of the house. He opened his door and got inside. He was about to start it, but before he put his key in the ignition, he noticed his car stereo was gone and that his steering column was popped.

"What the fuck?" he had yelled.

His mother came outside to see what had happened. "What's wrong?"

"Nothing, Mom. Go back in the house."

Ms. G was real nosey. Isaac automatically knew who the culprit was that had vandalized his car. He went inside the house and grabbed his mother's car keys. He came out of the house moving pretty fast and said, "Come on, Vic."

Raekwon got up, too, and they hopped in the car, driving off quickly.

In the car, Isaac was telling Vic that the Eses did it because the night before, he had thrown a Hennessey bottle at one of them for running into his car while trying to ride somebody on the handlebars of a low-rider bike.

The Eses had a little gang, and they would always get into it with them about something. They had shot a gage at Raekwon and Vic's houses before because Vic and Raekwon's brother Tip had gotten into it with them about something.

As they drove around looking for these dudes, Vic grew tired and told his brother that he wasn't going to find any of them. No sooner than he said that, Isaac spotted one on a mountain bike riding down Carson, Kel's block.

The Ese was halfway down the block and they were parked on the wrong side of the street, sitting in the car in front of Kel's house. Isaac put the car in drive and took off full speed. When the Ese noticed the car, he started peddling his bike like a bat out of hell. He was bobbing and weaving all through peoples' yards. He made a left on Randolph as they got closer and closer to him. Isaac turned the corner with no regards for life. The tires screeched. Isaac sped up finally catching up to the dude. The Ese tried to make a left on Blackhawk, but before he could turn, Isaac rammed the car into the back tire of the bike. The Ese flew off of the bike head first and landed on the driveway of the house that was at the corner. The garage door was open, so the Ese ran up in the garage and tried to go in the peoples' house, but the door was locked. He grabbed a shovel and stood at the top of the driveway swinging it as Isaac and Vic hopped out of the car to chase him down.

When Isaac grabbed the shovel out of the Ese's hands, he tried to run, but Vic tripped him, causing him to fall on his face. Vic and Isaac started kicking him until it looked like his face busted open.

"Don't you muthafuckas ever come stealing shit from me no more!" Isaac yelled.

Raekwon sat in the car watching like he was in the front-row seat at a 3D movie. That's the type of thing that usually happened when Raekwon was with them. They had a lot of excitement with them and nobody could tell them shit.

Raekwon explained to Vic and Raylin that his mother had just found out he was selling dope, and all they had to say to him was, "Don't even trip, homie. Just hit this weed."

When they got high, it was fun. They would just sit around and laugh while cracking jokes about everything. They didn't have a worry in the world when they were high.

Raekwon ended up kicking it over there until about the time Vic's mother was supposed to come home from work. After leaving there, he walked back around to the house and noticed his mother's car sitting in the driveway with a bunch of luggage inside it. He knew she didn't want him in the house. So, he just stood on the sidewalk in front of the house hoping that when she saw him, she would have some sympathy for him knowing that he didn't have a pot to piss in other than the one she provided for him.

The doors to the car were wide open, and the luggage filled the back seat, front seat, and the trunk. He was suspicious as to what was going on. Raekwon thought that maybe his mother and stepdad planned on moving without letting him know about it. The thought of that alone was enough to stir rage inside of him that would allow him to kill somebody and have no remorse about it.

"I want all of my shit!" Roxanne sounded as if she was yelling at the world.

"I don't give a damn what you take, as long as you don't take none of my shit wit' you!" Ben, Raekwon's stepdad, yelled back in a frustrated manner.

Raekwon was under the impression that his stepdad must have really pissed his mother off this time.

The screen door was propped open with a stick. Roxanne stepped out of the house with one of her plants in her hand and began to walk towards the car. Raekwon could tell just by looking at her expression that she was enraged. She went to the passenger side of the car and sat down. Raekwon noticed she acted as if she didn't even notice him when he knew she had.

Raekwon walked over to the passenger side of the car. Her face was planted in the palm of her hands.

"Momma, what's wrong?"

She didn't respond. She just began to cry a heavy cry that had the feeling of pain when it vibrated through his soul. Raekwon tried to pull one of her hands away from her face, but she only tensed up even more.

She spoke in a cry. "I'm tired. I'm tired. I'm just so tired of life." Her cries began to fade into deep sighs. "I can't take it no more, Lord. I just can't take it."

Raekwon ran in the house to grab her some tissue. When he came back out, he just stared at her and went into deep contemplation. There were more things going on in her life than he would ever know about.

"Where you goin'?" Raekwon decided to ask when he

noticed she was calming down.

"Why y'all doin' this to me?" She burst into tears again and sniffed in the running snot from the top of her lip. "Where is that stuff at?"

"I got rid of it." He had to lie, or it would have only made things worse.

Silence.

Raekwon asked again, "Where you goin'?"

"I'm moving to Memphis. Y'all don't love me because all y'all do to me is hurt me over and over again. I feel like everybody wanna just walk all over me. It's killing me, boy. I just can't do it no more. If it wasn't for God, I'd probably been done killed myself from puttin' up wit' y'all's mess."

"Don't go, Mom. We do care about you. I ain't trying to make things hard on you. Mom, please don't go. I love you."

That was the first time he had ever told his mother that he loved her, and it felt like he pushed a rock up out of his heart because he felt a lot lighter after that. He was shocked because he didn't feel it coming. He thought about it and knew it would change the scope of their mother-and-son relationship forever.

When they hugged, Roxanne cried tears of joy. He could tell she felt a little better after their conversation.

"You still leaving, Mom?"

"I'ma go over to Aunt Madison's house tonight so I can have some time to think about it, and I'll let you know in the morning."

With that said, she got in the driver's side, started up the car, backed out the driveway, and left.

Raekwon stared at the car until it disappeared like the sun behind the mountains. He was hurt. He never knew he could hurt his mother so deeply. He didn't place all of the blame on himself because he knew his stepdad had something to do with it, too.

The next morning, Roxanne called to see what was going on at the house. She had thought it out and had gotten the time and space that she needed. When he asked her when she was coming home, she told him that she was on her way. That's all he needed to know; he was secure.

Raekwon learned to be a little more responsible and realized he could really hurt someone else's feelings to the point of no return if the damage was irreparable. He started thinking more before he reacted.

CHAPTER 6

The dehydrated afternoon had started to come to an end. The sun had just begun to collapse behind the steep plateau. Raekwon was standing in the front doorway watching the sunset, when JC pulled up in front of the house in his Ford Taurus wagon. He stepped out of the car with a six pack of beers in his hand. When he looked up and saw Raekwon standing in the door, he nodded.

JC was stocky and dark-skinned with a perm that he always wore in a ponytail. His eyes were always red because he was always high. All he ever wore was Levis or Dickies. JC was gangbanging. He had about six gunshot wounds and had been stabbed in prison.

Raekwon stepped out onto the porch and nodded back.

"What's up, nigga?" he asked, holding his arms out as a welcome.

"What's happenin', lil homie?" JC responded, while approaching the front porch. "Where that nigga Tip at?"

"He just went to the liquor sto' wit' Juan. You can throw them brews in the freezer down in the basement if you want. I'll be down in a minute. I'm just waiting for somebody to slide through real quick."

When JC went downstairs, Raekwon walked in the kitchen and grabbed the cordless phone off of the table. He started to dial DG's number as he strolled back to the front door.

DG owned a record label. He had been admiring some of the music that Raekwon had let him hear a while ago and he wanted to sign him to his label. He told him that he was on his way over with the contract, but Raekwon was anxious to know why he was taking so long.

"Hello."

"What's up, nigga? Where you at?" Raekwon asked.

"Uhhh…" He hesitated then continued. "Over here off of Maxwell. You know a nigga be having a hard time finding his way through this side of town. I'ma be pullin' up in about five minutes."

"Alright then. I'll be sittin' on the front porch."

Raekwon began contemplating about his future. He knew he couldn't just live in the hood and sell dope all of his life. Everyone he ever knew that tried to do it that way turned into a dopefiend, got killed, or went to jail. He knew many that used the dope game as a way out, but it couldn't work for everybody. So, he was going to try his only other option…music.

DG pulled up in front of the driveway and turned off his headlights. He was driving a chameleon-green Monte Carlo on all-gold Daytons. He rolled down the passenger window and signaled for Raekwon to come to the car.

After Raekwon walked over and got in, he made eye contact with DG and gave him some dap. "What's up, man? What you been up to?" he asked.

He took a deep breath and replied, "Man, I just been

grindin' and tryin' to finish up this new album I been workin' on."

Album, Raekwon thought. He always wanted to put out his own album. He gave DG a stately look and drifted off into a daze until DG tapped him on the shoulder with the back of his hand and asked, "You ready to look at that thang and sign it?"

"Yeah," Raekwon responded, assuring him with a smile. "Where that muthafucka at?"

DG reached in his backseat and grabbed a black briefcase. He put the briefcase on his lap, opened it, and started fumbling through some papers.

Raekwon acted like he was looking out the window, but actually, he had his eyes cut towards the contents of the briefcase. He frequently looked to try to read DG's facial expression because he didn't know why, but he had a funny feeling about the whole situation.

After skimming some papers, DG handed them over to Raekwon and said, "Here, you can read it if you want, but all it's sayin' is that the deal is for two years and that you agree to percentages."

Raekwon looked at the paper, then looked at DG. He raised his left eyebrow and asked, "What percent do you get?"

"I get thirty percent," he replied in a nonchalant way while counting a stack of money.

"How come you get thirty and I only get twenty when I'm making all of my own music?" Raekwon asked with a skeptical look.

DG returned a serious look and said, "Well, you know I'm putting up all of the money to put yo' shit out. Plus, I gotta spend a reasonable piece of change to promote it, too."

Raekwon's curiosity level came down some after DG brought up the expenses, because what he was saying made some sense to him. He always heard people talking about how you had to be careful when you're doing business with individuals because they will get over on you if you let them. He was trying to be cautious and see if that was the case.

DG closed his briefcase and rolled up a blunt of indo on top of it. He then pulled out a pint of Hennessy from underneath his seat. He set the contract down on his lap, opened up the bottle of yak, took a short swallow, and then handed the bottle to Raekwon, who took a sip and passed it back.

DG held the bottle up to the car's interior light and said, "Damn, nigga, you ain't even put a dent in this shit." He looked at Raekwon and tried to hand the bottle back. "You want some mo'?" he asked.

"Naw, I'm cool," Raekwon responded in a nonchalant manner.

DG lit the weed and cracked the window open on the driver's side. After hitting it a couple of times, he asked him, "You need a pen so you can sign that shit?"

Raekwon gave him an uncertain look before replying, "Uhh...yeah, let me see one real quick."

DG started coughing. "Damn!" He grabbed his chest. "This some bomb-ass weed." He held the blunt out towards Raekwon and said, "Here, nigga, hit this shit."

As soon as he took his first hit, he started coughing. "Damn! This shit is fire," Raekwon said in-between coughs.

Hrrrrat! Hrrrat! Harrat! The sound of gunshots echoed from a couple of blocks away. Raekwon and DG exchanged wide-eyed looks.

DG asked, "You hear that shit?" He quickly opened his briefcase and grabbed an ink pen. "Here, man," he said, while handing it to him. "Hurry up and sign that shit so I can bounce before the police be everywhere." He then reached in-between his seat and pulled out a quarter ounce of dope. "Here, you can have this shit. I ain't tryin to get pulled over wit' no dope on me."

Raekwon grabbed the dope and put it in his pocket. "Good lookin', nigga." He then grabbed the ink pen and signed the contract.

After he finished signing the contract, he and DG shook hands before he got out of the car. JC was standing on the front porch with a beer in his hand and an awkward look on his face.

JC stepped off of the porch and said, "For a minute, I thought some shit was goin' down out here, nigga. I was sittin' in the kitchen talkin' to my bitch and it sounded like I heard somebody bustin' a heat."

Raekwon gave JC a serious look. "Shit, somebody *was* shootin'. It was somewhere around the corner. It sounded like it came from over there by the park or somethin'."

Tip and Juan suddenly came accelerating from around the corner and barged into the driveway. Both of them hurried out of the car, slamming the doors.

"What y'all niggas done did?" Raekwon asked.

"We ain't did shit," Juan answered. "Niggas just see the police swoopin' everywhere. Shit, I got warrants and ain't got no license or nothin'. I had to smash out on the muthafuckas 'cause they hit the block and started lookin' at us when they passed by us."

"Somebody just got through shootin'." Raekwon gave Tip

and Juan a dubious look and continued. "And I thought y'all niggas did that shit by the way y'all came flying up the block."

Tip inquired, "Somebody was shootin'?"

"Hell yeah, somebody—" JC was interrupted by the sound of his pager beeping. After he looked at it, he said, "Let me get this phone real quick 'cause somebody's paging me from around the corner at Keelan's house wit' nine-one-one."

After Juan grabbed the liquor out of the car, they all went inside of the house. JC stopped in the kitchen to use the phone, while the rest of them made their way towards the stairs.

Before Raekwon turned into the stairway that led to the basement, he noticed a strange look on JC's face. "You think everything is okay wit' that nigga?" he asked him.

"I don't know," JC said, "but that shit just doesn't seem right for nobody to be leaving that code in my shit from over there."

"Shit! Well, I'm 'bout to go put this dope up and grab me a drink, homie." Raekwon then headed down the stairs.

After about five minutes, JC came downstairs with his gun in his hand. Tip, Juan, and Raekwon gave him curious looks. Raekwon eased off of the couch and started to walk towards him.

"Damn!" JC shouted after lifting his head up and revealing his bloodshot eyes.

"What's wrong, nigga?" Raekwon asked.

JC sighed. "I just talked to Keelan's broad, and she said he just got smoked by some niggas in a dark-colored compact car with no license plates. She said they shot the nigga like six or seven times with a fully-loaded automatic."

Raekwon looked at JC in disbelief. "Is that right?"

"Yeah, nigga, that shit is a trip." JC shook his head and continued. "That was the shots we heard a couple of blocks over about forty-five minutes ago. I just left from over there with him and Black Eddy before I came over here."

"That was over there by where we seen them police, too," Tip added.

JC looked at Raekwon. "Would you take me over there to that nigga Black Eddy's house?" he asked, while putting his pistol in his waistline.

Raekwon starred at JC and stroked his chin as he gave his question some thought. He didn't want to have any run-in with the police because he didn't have his license and his taillight was busted out. He also didn't want to deny his friend a ride in a serious situation.

Keelan and JC were from the same gang. So, he could only imagine how devastated JC must have been. JC and Keelan had a baby by the same broad. Black Eddy, JC, and Keelan were road dogs and always rolled together.

Sensing Raekwon's hesitation, JC turned to Juan. "Nigga, take me over there to Black Ed's real fast."

"Man, I just got out of the streets tryin' to avoid getting picked up for these warrants I got," Juan told him.

"Shit, I got warrants, too," JC replied, raising his voice. "I just don't want to drive my shit 'cause I got nine ounces stashed in my shit."

"Fuck it, nigga. Let's roll," Raekwon finally said. "But you gonna have to lock yo' pistol in my glove box."

JC agreed and they started walking towards the stairs.

When they got inside Raekwon's car, he made sure JC put his pistol in the glove box before he pulled off. He got butterflies in his stomach as he adjusted his seat and pressed down on the gas pedal.

"So that nigga's broad don't know who smoked him?"

"Naw, the bitch said she was just coming out of the bathroom and Keelan was in front of the house. She said the car was about halfway down the block when she got to the front door."

They drove in silence for a couple of blocks until they got by Black Eddy's house. When Raekwon started to turn on the street, he noticed a police car sitting in the parking lot of The Market with their lights off.

"Damn!"

"Yeah," JC said, "I saw them muthafuckas over there, too. Fuck 'em. Just hit the block, bust a U-turn, and park right across the street from Black Ed's house."

After Raekwon parked, he turned off the headlights. JC got out of the car and walked up to Black Eddy's front door. When JC went inside, Raekwon noticed the headlights on the police car had turned on.

"Fuck!" Raekwon said out loud to himself as he began to slide down in his seat.

The patrol car pulled out of the parking lot and started up Black Eddy's street. As they approached Raekwon's car, they slowed down and shined the spotlight through the window. His heart skipped a beat when he saw the two cops with devious looks on their faces.

His cold sweat quickly disappeared when the patrol car kept going. He watched in his rearview mirror as they continued to drive up the street and around the curve that defined the narrow block.

After a couple of minutes passed, JC emerged from the house with a blank look on his face. As he was crossing the street to approach the car, Raekwon noticed the rev of an engine catch his attention, causing him to stop in his tracks.

Raekwon looked over his shoulder and noticed the same police car that had passed by minutes before was quickly pulling up in front of JC with their lights off. The patrol car sounded a quick siren and turned on their spotlight.

JC stood in the middle of the street with a puzzled look on his face, while both of the officers stepped out of the car. Raekwon noticed that Officer Vamadier had been driving and had a rookie with him. Vamadier had been chasing them out of crack houses for the past two or three years. They considered Vamadier to be a blood-sucking white man. So, in the streets, he was referred to as Vamp, a nickname he soon got used to.

When the rookie came and tapped on Raekwon's window with his flashlight, Raekwon rolled down his window and gave him a stupefied look.

"Step out of the car, sir," the rookie said in a demanding voice.

"How y'all gonna pull me over and I'm parked?"

The Vamp replied, "If your damn taillight wasn't busted, I probably wouldn't have even recognized the car."

The Vamp made them lean forward over the trunk of the police car with their hands behind their backs, while the rookie searched Raekwon's car.

Backing out of Raekwon's car, the rookie looked at Vamp and said, "I can't get the fucking glove compartment open." He then looked at Raekwon and asked, "Where's the key to your glove box?"

"I ain't got no key to it, and that glove box is broke anyway," he lied convincingly. Actually, he had the key in the sole of his shoe and was hoping they wouldn't search him.

"What the fuck y'all fuckin' wit us fo' anyway? We ain't even did shit," JC exclaimed with frustration in his voice.

The Vamp grabbed his belt with both hands and pulled up his pants like a cowboy. He walked towards JC and said, "Don't play stupid, Mr. Jabar Coleman. Now, if you're buddy Keelan Ferguson didn't get murdered tonight, you probably wouldn't have me thinking you're out to retaliate."

"Man, I don't know what the fuck you talkin' 'bout."

"Yes, you do," Vamp said. "I'm pretty sure you're able to tell us who killed your friend so we can save you guys from being in their situation."

JC didn't respond. Insitead, he just gave Vamp a cold stare and sighed.

Vamp looked toward the rookie officer. "Keep an eye on these two while I go run warrants on 'em.

While Vamp sat in his patrol car, the rookie watched them closely while gripping the pistol that sat in his holster.

A second police car hit the block and pulled up to Vamp's window. Vamp stepped out of the car and walked around to where JC and Raekwon were still leaning against the patrol car. As he stepped closer to JC, he began to pull out his handcuffs. He told the rookie to cuff Raekwon and put him in the back of the other patrol car.

Raekwon asked, "What the fuck is goin' on?"

"The homicide detective wants to ask you two a couple of questions," Vamp responded without making eye contact with him.

Before Raekwon got a chance to say anything else, the rookie stuffed him in the backseat of the patrol car. He shook his head in disbelief and sighed.

After a long trip across town, they arrived downtown at the police headquarters. After punching in a code, the officer pulled down into the underground police garage. There were all kinds of unmarked vehicles that Raekwon had seen before. He was very familiar with the police headquarters because he had been booked in juvenile intake more times than he could remember.

As they stepped inside of the elevator, he became a little nervous. Raekwon had seen the other police car pull up with JC in it, but he was wondering why the two weren't put on the elevator together. The elevator was quiet. The butterflies revisited his stomach once again as the elevator doors opened up on the seventh floor.

There stood a chubby white man with a beer belly. He had a full beard, and he wore glasses and a toupee. He had on a light blue dress shirt with the sleeves rolled up to his elbows. He had on some black slacks that were pulled up to his stomach and held in place by some red suspenders.

When one of the officers finally removed the handcuffs from Raekwon, he massaged both of his wrists and held a resentful look on his face.

The pudgy white man held out his hand and said, "Hi, I'm Detective Winthorne."

Raekwon looked at him like he was stupid and put his hands in his pocket. He was taught to never shake a cop's hand.

Winthorne smirked. "I understand you're frustrated, but this won't take long."

He took Raekwon to a room that didn't have a window on

the door. The only things inside of the room were a table and three chairs.

"Have a seat over there," Winthorne said, while pointing to the chair on the other side of the table.

After Raekwon sat down, chills ran through his body from the cold air blowing out of the vents. He looked around and sighed. *This is a trip,* he thought.

Winthorne leaned forward, rested both hands on the table, and gave him a discerning look. "So where were you when Mr. Ferguson was gunned down?"

"I don' know what the fuck you talking about. I ain't know nothin' 'bout nobody gettin' killed," Raekwon lied with a credible look on his face.

For about thirty minutes, Winthorne asked Raekwon questions that he wouldn't have given him answers to even if he did know. After Raekwon grew tired from the questioning, he laid his head on the table and ignored him. When Detective Winthorne finally accepted the fact that he wasn't going to get any answers out of him, he let Raekwon use the phone to call for someone to pick him up.

Raekwon stood outside of the police station waiting for his ride. The police had thrown JC in jail for some traffic warrants he had. Raekwon was glad he was able to squeeze his way out of the situation without too many problems.

When Tip pulled up in Juan's car, he felt relieved. Raekwon walked up to the car and hopped in. During the drive back to town, he told Tip everything that had happened when he and JC left the house. Tip was paranoid the whole way back, hoping he wouldn't get pulled over, too.

After Tip dropped Raekwon off at his car, Raekwon drove

over to Tone's house.

Raekwon met Tone through his sister that he used to mess with a couple of years back. Tone was about ten years older than he. When Raekwon was growing up, he used to always see him driving through town in his convertible Caprice on chrome Daytons and hydraulics. Raekwon always knew he was a hustler, but his first conversation with him was about music. He was doing his thing with music, but Raekwon knew selling dope was his priority at the time.

After a couple of knocks, Tone finally answered the door and let him in. He was playing John Madden football on his Playstation and smoking on a blunt.

"What's up wit' you, lil nigga?" Tone asked.

"Man, just a whole bunch of bullshit."

He told him about Keelan getting killed, and how he and JC got taken down for questioning against their will.

Tone hit the blunt and said, "Yeah, I just heard about that nigga Keelan about an hour ago." He passed him the weed.

After Raekwon told Tone about the contract from DG that he had signed, Tone had a strange reaction, which confirmed the uneasy feeling Raekwon felt when he was sitting in the car with DG.

Tone gave him a shameful look. "Why you fuckin' wit' that scary-ass nigga? I remember when that nigga got knocked out and punked for his dope spot."

"Oh yeah?"

"Yeah," Tone confirmed. "That nigga's a mark." Tone took a swig of the beer that sat on the table and then asked, "What did the contract say?"

Raekwon stroked his chin and replied, "It said I get twenty

percent of all the—"

Tone cut him off. "Twenty percent?! So that means that nigga gets the other eighty percent."

He looked at Tone strangely. "What you mean eighty? He said he gets thirty."

"Man, don't fall for that bullshit." Tone stood up and gave him a serious look. "It's a hundred percent in every percentage scale, lil homie. Was yo' mom there when you signed it?"

"Naw, why?"

"That shit ain't no good then 'cause you're only fifteen years old," Tone told him. "You gotta be at least eighteen to sign some shit like that without a legal guardian. That nigga had to know that shit. You need to call that nigga right now and tell him what I just told you."

Raekwon ended up getting out of the record contract with DG and destroying whatever business relationship he had built with him. He was glad Tone warned him before it was too late. The only problem was that Raekwon lost hope and drifted deeper in the streets.

CHAPTER 7

It was about five thirty in the afternoon when Raekwon's homeboy, Donnie, pulled up in a car that they always rented from a dopefiend. It was a maroon Seville with a moonroof. He had been standing outside drinking on a beer, waiting for him to come and pick him up so they could hook up with some broads that Donnie knew.

Donnie was one of Raekwon's hustling partners, and they would usually go kick it with broads together, too. Donnie was a light-skinned, laidback dude. His pops was a drunk that drove a beat-up Lincoln with beer cans and trash always over the seats and floor. His pops was a dopefiend but thought Donnie didn't know about it.

After Raekwon hopped in the car, Donnie sped off. The interior smelled like a flower garden. Raekwon could tell he had gone by the carwash, vacuumed it out, and bought the cherry incense that was hanging from the gear shifter.

"Damn, nigga, you sho' got this muthafucka smellin' spiffy," Raekwon said, while rolling down the window.

Donnie gave a one-sided grin. "Well, you know bitches love the consideration of a young man's upbringing. I like to keep these dandelions watered with fresh memories in case I have to dig 'em out in the backseat or something'."

The look that Raekwon gave him told him to knock it off. Raekwon grabbed his case of CD's and began to look through them. After he popped in Mr. Mike's first album, they both started head-bobbing.

"Hey, what's up with the LQ?" Raekwon had turned down the volume of the stereo to ask the question.

Donnie leaned back with one hand on the steering wheel like he was a Mack. "Don't even trip, homie." He used his other hand to lift up the armrest and reveal a pint of Remy Martin. "I got two, thirty-two ounces of Old-E under the seat, too."

Raekwon grabbed the Remy, cracked it open, and took a swig. "Hey, fool, you got yo' cell phone wit' you?"

Donnie pointed towards the glove compartment. "Aw yeah, that muthafucka's right up in there."

He had one of those bulky, old-school cell phones that you couldn't even fit in your pocket. He got it from a dopefiend for thirty dollars' worth of dope, and it had already been on for two months.

Raekwon plugged the cord in the car lighter and got the number from Donnie to call the broads to let them know they were on their way. Donnie had a joint sitting on the edge of the ashtray. When Raekwon reached for it, it slid down into a pile of ashes. He dug his fingers in to grab the joint and felt something little, round, and hard. He frowned up like he had stuck his hand in some dog feces.

"Aw, shit!" Raekwon yelled, snatching his hand back.

Donnie looked at him funny. "What happened, fool?"

He reached back in the ashtray and pulled out the crack pipe that was stuffed in the back of it. He shook his head. "Boy, I tell you. These baseheads'll leave this shit layin' around anywhere."

Raekwon threw it out the window and lit up the weed.

***

Raekwon was sitting on the couch high as hell. The broad that Donnie hooked him up with was sitting on the chair holding the cordless phone in her hand and acting like she was on some stubborn shit. Donnie was somewhere upstairs with the other broad.

Raekwon cut his eyes towards Natalie, licked his lips, and asked, "So what's up wit' you?"

She didn't have any shoes on and her feet were tucked up under her. She bit the corner of her bottom lip and gave him a guilty look. "Waiting for my nigga to call me."

Raekwon thought to himself, *This stupid-ass bitch got me on a dummy mission.* He paused to catch his reckless thoughts, and then said, "Oh yeah? Why you have me come over here if you was gonna be sittin' around waitin' for your nigga to call?"

"Damn, nigga, you sho' is askin' a lot of questions. I ain't the one who wanted to kick it wit' you, homeboy."

Shaking his head, Raekwon stood up and exclaimed, "Y'all some stupid-ass broads."

Natalie tried to get some heart. "Broads? Nigga, I ain't no muthafuckin' broad. You—"

Raekwon cut her off. "Shut the fuck up!"

"Nigga, you shut the fuck up!"

Obviously, Donnie and Sheila heard all of the commotion because they came downstairs.

Donnie asked, "What's wrong, homie?"

"These lil' hoes is on some bullshit, and I'm ready to go," Raekwon exclaimed stubbornly.

Both of the girls started talking so much that they couldn't really hear what they were saying. All Raekwon knew was that everybody took sides. So, he and Donnie ended up cussed them out and leaving.

For some odd reason, Raekwon always had a bitter attitude towards women. Maybe it was because that's with whom almost all of his encounters were with. He always got into disagreements with his mother, aunts, teachers, and smart-mouthed broads around the neighborhood. He had very little respect and sometimes no respect at all.

As they drove back to town, it began to get dark. They had to go and drop the car back off to the dopefiend who had been paging Donnie, but Donnie didn't bother to return his calls. Most likely, the dopefiend had run out of dope and was calling to try to convince Donnie to give him a couple of more crumbs when he dropped the car off.

They had planned on going to a get-together that a lot of people they knew were going to be at. Some females they knew were the ones putting it together. So, Raekwon had to go and pull his car out of retirement, which was something he didn't want to do. He was trying to keep from driving his car because he knew the next time the police caught him in it, they were going to take it. Raekwon was thinking about his last run-in where he got into a high-speed chase.

He remembered hopping into the car with Carlos and another one of his partners that he grew up with. He wanted to show them how much smash his car had and how it floated across the gravel like a spaceship. At least, he thought so.

They hit a couple of corners, and every time he got enough lane to work with, he punched it, pressing the pedal to the floor. He came off of Chandler Street and turned left, screeching onto Randolph.

The police happened to be four blocks up, coming straight towards them. Handling this type of situation was nothing new to him. He knew exactly what to do. Raekwon made a quick left on Blackhawk and pressed all the way down on the gas. The car jerked and the engine roared a little louder as he gained speed. As he was approaching Billings Street, he began to slow down to make the turn, while Carlos looked back to see how close the police were behind them. Carlos informed Raekwon that the police were picking up speed. Raekwon kept hitting block after block, hoping to lose them.

Raekwon knew the lefts and rights of The Maze with his eyes closed. These were the blocks he grew up on, the blocks that he learned how to sell dope on, the streets where there were no alleyways. That's where it all went down. He lived in the backstreets of The Maze, where it was everything but a peaceful place to live.

After hitting so many blocks and running so many stop signs, he thought he had gotten away. So, he decided to turn onto a main street.

There they were. The front end of the police car was damn near peeking around the corner about six blocks down. As soon as he noticed it, he punched out at high speed, making a right on the first block he came to.

The chase went on. All they could think about was getting away. Raekwon wasn't nervous, but his adrenaline was rushing from the excitement of the thrill. Everybody in the car was holding on to the seats. The tires were screeching at every corner he turned. As he approached Xanadu Street and prepared to make a wide left turn, Carlos told him the police were getting closer.

Raekwon failed to slow down enough to make the turn and almost crashed into a boat that some white people were standing around. Finally, he was nervous at that point because he thought he was going to jail. He still didn't think they could catch him, though. He felt like he was untouchable.

Raekwon came to a screeching stop and quickly put the car in reverse. As he was backing up, he noticed the police car flying up towards the corner he'd just turned off of. That's when a big, country-looking white man dressed in overalls came running towards Raekwon's car as if he was trying to save the day.

He sped off and the chase was back on again. The only difference this time was the police were on his tail now. The only way he was going to get away was if he were to hop out of the car. So, that's exactly what he did.

Raekwon ended up having to get his car out of the pound a couple days later. He learned a big lesson from that experience. Stay out of the way.

Donnie interrupted his daydream by asking him if he still wanted to go to the get-together. Once again, Raekwon didn't really want to drive his car, but being drunk, he looked at him and said, "Shit, fuck it, nigga. Let's mob."

Donnie took a swig of his beer. "You wanna go get some 'A'?"

Raekwon gave him a crazy look like he had just insulted him. "Hell naw! Nigga, I'm cool on that shit."

He wasn't trying to take no acid, even though it was the drug of choice in the town at the time. The last time Raekwon had taken some acid, he must have thought he was Superman or some other superhero. After that experience, he told himself that he would never take that shit ever again.

He remembered the incident clearly. Raekwon was with LP. They hit up one of the neighborhood dope houses to grab a couple hits of acid and a bag of skunk weed. They rode their stolen mountain bikes, the ones they went everywhere on. That's how they got around the hood from spot to spot.

Raekwon expected the acid to hit him right away like some weed or liquor, but it didn't. He started to think it was some bullshit and chalked it up as a loss as if he had gotten beat out of some money.

They ended up going over some female's house named Candy, who always had some of her homegirls over. Candy would never give the homies any pussy, but her friends were some freaks.

LP ended up going home because he was on house arrest and had to be home when his P.O. called. Their homeboy Big Tiny had already been over there when they got to Candy's. They ended up raiding her refrigerator, her momma's jewelry box, and whatever else there was for them to get into. They stayed on some bullshit whenever they went to Candy's house. She hated them, but she loved their company.

Raekwon was in the living room trying to push up on Candy, and when she rejected his advances, he told her that he was about to go downstairs to her room. She didn't like for anyone to be in her room. So, she chased him through the kitchen, but she stopped at the top of the stairs as he rushed down them, skipping steps. Candy decided to get Big Tiny out of her refrigerator rather than chase Raekwon around the house. He heard her yelling at Big Tiny, telling him to leave.

Raekwon ended up in the basement by himself. He picked up one of her little brother's toy Uzi from the middle of the floor. It was Raekwon's reaction to his fascination with guns. He then walked into Candy's room and dove onto her waterbed.

Raekwon laid back and stared at the ceiling, while pulling the trigger of the toy. All he was focused on was the random clicking noises it made. All of a sudden, it felt like the water turned to quicksand and seemed like the sounds of the toy Uzi came to life. The gun started speaking in tongues as if it were really loaded.

Raekwon dropped the gun and hopped up out the bed. He ran up the stairs and out the door without saying a word. Then he hopped on his stolen transportation and rode around towards LP's house. As he rode, he felt a burst of reckless energy. That's when he realized the acid had kicked in. He had forgotten about it for a while, but now, he was feeling the effects of it.

When he got to LP's house, he was in the backyard burning up some hotdogs on the bar-b-que grill. Kemo and Big Tiny came jumping fences into LP's backyard. They had a little trail the dopefiends used when they sat back there and sold dope.

Raekwon heard Big Vic pull up around the front. He knew it was him by the way the car stereo sounded in his brother's car. Vic walked into the backyard smoking a blunt.

LP started eating the burnt hot dogs straight off the grill, without bread. He looked like a pit bull the way food was falling out of his mouth. It was obvious Raekwon and LP was on some type of dope because they joined in.

Kemo, Tiny, and Vick stared at them like they were crazy. LP was chasing Kemo all over the backyard like he was trying to bite him, while Kemo escaped him by hopping into yards that he knew would set off LP's house arrest band if he followed.

Kemo hopped back in the yard and ran to the pine tree that was by the fence. He grabbed a Doritos bag from underneath it, and from the bag, he produced a rusty .380 pistol. LP stopped chasing him and started cussing him out for hiding the pistol in his backyard. The joke was over.

"That must be some good shit," Vic said. "Did y'all get that shit from them muthafuckas over there on Carlos' block?"

Raekwon didn't know what they put in it, but he didn't even get tired.

Sometime around one o'clock in the morning, Raekwon and Vic ended up walking back over to LP's house because they couldn't sleep. They knew he had to be up, too. When they finally got there, there was a dopefiend standing in his front yard at his bedroom window. They ended up beating the basehead's ass and chilling with LP until the sun came up. Raekwon didn't want to experience that ever again.

After Donnie dropped off the dopefiend's car, they asked him to drop them off at Raekwon's house. Just as they figured, the dopefiend wanted Donnie to give him another piece of crack. He begged and pleaded until Donnie finally had some sympathy for him. Since he was a loyal customer, that's the only reason Donnie looked out for him.

When the dopefiend reached into his ashtray, Raekwon knew exactly what he was looking for, but he didn't say anything. He had one hand on the steering wheel and the other hand searching for the crack pipe in a panic.

Donnie looked at the fiend with an irritated cold stare. "If you're lookin' for that punk-ass pipe, we threw that muthafucka out the window. Nigga, you be on some reckless shit. We could have gotten caught up if the police woulda pulled us over." Donnie sighed and shook his head. "I hope you didn't think you was gonna smoke that shit wit' us in the car anyway."

The fiend's eyes got big as if he was nervous. "Naw...naw, man...my bad...my bad," he stuttered. "I just gotta hurry up and meet somebody. Uh, where y'all goin'? Where y'all goin'?" he asked uneasily.

He wasn't making any sense, but he did manage to get them to Raekwon's house without any drama.

When they pulled up to the party, cars were everywhere. Raekwon could see people packing into the backyard from a distance. Although he was already tipsy, he was still trying to drink a little more.

When Donnie and Raekwon stepped in, they spotted a couple of homies in the back corner of the yard over by the gate. Raekwon could tell they were getting high. They walked over to the corner where they were chilling. They had two gallons of Carlos Rossi, and Kel was clutching his own personal pint of gin.

Raekwon started scoping the crowd so see who all was on the scene. There were a couple of broads that he had been digging, but Camilla was there, too, and she was hurting them. Her hair was freshly cut into a bob style, which was perfect on her. He couldn't keep his eyes off of her. He couldn't resist it, so he strolled up to speak to her for a minute.

"What's happenin' wit' you, girl?" He stroked his chin and

looked her up and down. "I see you're lookin' good as always."

She gave him a seductive smile. "I'm fine, and thank you."

"How long you been here?" he asked.

"Not long. Probably about thirty minutes."

He knew she could tell he was drunk because he saw it in her facial expression.

It was something about her that drew him to her like a magnet, but he started to get sloppy with his approach. His conversation began to get bland. He didn't know why, but he froze every time he really wanted to spit at her with some of his strongest game. She knew what his lifestyle was like, and he always had the feeling she wouldn't accept him as her man because of the fact that he was labeled a hoodlum.

He went back to where the homies were standing at and played the background. They smoked a little weed and drank a little more. He wasn't really big on dancing. He just liked the atmosphere. Damn near every nigga he knew up in there was on acid.

The homie Pokey was on Sherm, like always. He had been starting to lose a lot of sense lately. He was a straight fool about his. About a month back, Pokey went to a dopefiend's house tripping about twenty-five dollars that the dopefiend had owed him. The dopefiend ended up knocking Pokey's tooth out, and he beat the shit out of the basehead.

Everywhere Pokey went, he was always driving at high-speed and outrunning the police. He was a speed demon.

Suddenly, there was some commotion going on in the front of the house. When Raekwon and Donnie rushed through the gate to see what was going on, they found Davon in the front yard making a scene, calling his girl all kinds of bitches for conversation with other dudes.

Davon was wild, bold, and acted like he never thought about the consequences to anything he did. He lived with his grandmother because his mother abandoned him and his brother, Will. He was always fighting with somebody or starting some trouble, and when something went down, he would always come by Raekwon's house to borrow his pistol. Raekwon used to go and sleep in Davon and Will's grandma's broken-down van sometimes when his mother would kick him out of the house.

Davon's girl was Bodine's sister, and Bodine's house was a hangout spot. With all the dudes that hung out there, his house was targeted and raided twice by the task force. They had guns to Bodine's little sisters' heads and stripped them naked to see if there were any drugs being hidden on them. That's something that would have them traumatized for the rest of their lives.

"Bitch-ass nigga, don't be disrespectin' my sister. I don't give a fuck if she yo' girl or not!" Bodine was furious.

Davon took off his shirt. He was drunk and gone off of acid. "What's up then, punk-ass nigga?"

As they both started to square up, Will tried to jump in and help his brother. Bodine's sister ran up on Davon, swinging and screaming.

"Get yo' ass out the way!" Bodine yelled at his sister.

"Fuck that bitch! Let her come on," Davon said sarcastically.

Will grabbed Davon from behind. "Chill out, nigga."

Davon jerked away. "Get the fuck off of me, nigga."

When people started saying that somebody had called the police, Raekwon went and sat in his car to watch what was going on. He looked around for Donnie, but he didn't see him. When he looked back over to where the drama was playing out, Davon was squared up with his brother Will. That's when Raekwon finally spotted Donnie. He was trying to break the shit up.

Raekwon hated what he was seeing. The whole situation made him look stupid, too, because these were dudes that he ran the streets with sometimes. He grew furious as the scene got out of hand. Unable to control himself, he grabbed his pistol from under the seat, pointed it in the air, and let off two shots.

People started scattering, diving on the ground, and sliding under cars. Raekwon heard tires peeling off and people yelling and screaming.

Donnie, Bodine, Ty, and his cousin Kendu hopped in Raekwon's car, and he peeled off. He didn't even bother to turn on his headlights. He was a little nervous, and the only thing on his mind was getting away. He was afraid somebody was going to snitch and tell the police that he was the one shooting. His foot was all the way down on the pedal as he approached an intersection.

"Hey, nigga, watch out!" Kendu yelled.

Raekwon's adrenaline raced through his veins as he spotted the car entering the four-way intersection in front of him. He pressed the brakes as hard as he could, and his car fishtailed as he tried to gain control of it. The car abruptly ran up on the sidewalk and ripped through a wooden fence that surrounded the backyard of a house that was on the corner.

They suddenly stopped. Raekwon thought they were about

to die. He peeked over the steering wheel and saw all of the damage he had done to the people's yard. He didn't care if the car was wrecked or not; he just wanted to get away.

He tried to start the car but no luck. He was a little nervous because he didn't want to have to face the owner of the house, and most of all, he didn't want to deal with the police. The good thing was that the whole time he watched the back door of the house, nobody ever looked out or came outside.

After he popped the hood, Kendo figured out that the car's battery was what was stalling their getaway. They finally got back in traffic at high speed. Raekwon quickly dropped Tee and Kendo off, and then he sped all the way to the house and parked in the backyard.

He, Donnie, and Bodine walked down to Raylin's house where they noticed some dudes standing outside.

"What's up wit' y'all niggas?" Raekwon asked as they walked up into the open garage.

Raylin's brother, Saul, was sitting in the garage drinking some beers with some of his homies. Saul looked at Raekwon like he noticed something suspicious.

"What's up wit' y'all? Where's my brother at?"

Raekwon gave Saul a blank look. "Shit, I thought—"

Raekwon bit his tongue after noticing the police car hit the block and drive by slowly. Raekwon, Donnie, and Bodine slipped into the backyard and were standing close by the fence prepared to jump if the police stopped and got out of the car. The police slowed down by the house, flashed the spotlight on it, and then kept going.

GoGo came into the backyard and asked, "What y'all lil' niggas done did?"

After they told him about the incident at the party, GoGo told Raekwon to go inside of the house and put some bleach on his arms. He said the bleach would get rid of the gun powder that was on his skin.

They ended up staying in the garage for the rest of the night getting drunk. Bodine got so drunk that they had to wheel him home in one of the city trashcans because everyone who had cars had already left. Raekwon damn sure wasn't going to drive his car to take him home. They laughed the whole way to Bodine's house.

It was a trip how the days came and went by so fast. Raekwon was so busy in his distorted view of the world that he couldn't notice his flaws. He had a feeling that something or somebody was out to get him caught up in some shit.

Even though his mother didn't condone the way he was living, she still showed him that she loved him. She would sometimes, out of the blue, come in the basement with a bottle of prayer oil, put some on her son's forehead, and pray for him right where he sat or stood. Raekwon believed in God, and he knew He had a plan for him; but what it was, he had no idea.

CHAPTER 8

Raekwon's pager vibrated for the sixth time. He got up and told Ms. Monroe, his math teacher, that he had to use the restroom. He hated math, especially if it didn't have anything to do with counting money. Shit, he hated school if it didn't have anything to do with dissecting reptiles or ditching class in the halls.

On his way to the bathroom, he checked his pager. It read: 007-40-007-911. He knew it was Mary by the code, and that's all it was…a code and no number. She agreed to never leave her phone number for a very good reason. Raekwon always got sweated by the police about specific phone numbers in his pager whenever he got hemmed up, especially if the phone number was followed by a dollar amount.

Mary was a regular customer. Her husband sold weed, and she would always steal sacks from him and trade them for half of the amount they were worth for crack.

Raekwon never went back inside the classroom, he just left. He did that a lot whenever he went to math class because Ms. Monroe wanted him to kiss her ass just to get her to help him with what they were learning. He wasn't going to pass anyway because he had too many absences. He just went to school to see the females and kick it with the homies.

When he walked up to The Market to use the phone, there were a couple of dudes that he knew from around the way standing outside of the store. They were the usual crowd. Most of them never even made it to school in the morning. It seemed like they just got dressed, went up to the store, and stayed there smoking and drinking all day.

Mary pulled up to the store in her raggedy Delta eighty-eight. The paint on the car was chipped in some places and faded in others. Being a short, white lady who always wore sunglasses, she always had a suspicious look about her.

Raekwon halfway trusted Mary because he'd been dealing with her for over a year now. She would sometimes page him just to let him know that the police, whom she referred to as They Boys, were in the vicinity. He respected her natural integrity.

He hopped inside the car and they drove off.

"Damn, you was blowin' my pager up. I hope you got some money this time, because I walked out of class and got ran off the school property by them punk-ass security guards," Raekwon said, adding extra to the story.

She looked at him real quick with a one-sided grin and turned back so she wouldn't end up running off the road. "Come on now. You could at least give me more credit than that. You know I wouldn't shit you."

"Credit? I ain't givin' out no credit today," he joked about her comment.

Once they pulled up to her house, they went inside. Her house smelled like wet dogs. They had two dirty-ass fishtanks with a couple of goldfish in them. In the kitchen, there was a small television sitting on the counter. On the kitchen table were backdated newspapers, magazines, and mail. There was also an empty breadbox.

Raekwon sat down and looked around. He hadn't been inside their house in about a month because he always had Mary pick him up off of some corner whenever they made a transaction.

"Hey, you wanna trade a twenty?" Mary yelled from her room.

"I thought you said you had some money?" he asked sarcastically with a touch of frustration in his voice.

"A friend of mine wanted a forty, and she's on her way over here right now. I wanted to trade some smoke to you so I could have a little something for myself, too."

A car horn honked outside, and Mary peeked out of the curtains. "That's her right there." She got the dope from Raekwon and went outside. When she came back, she traded him some weed for some dope.

Mary stood on the tips of her toes while reaching on top of the refrigerator. She pulled down a glass pipe and began putting a small piece of dope in it.

"What the fuck is you doin'? Don't smoke that shit around me!" Raekwon reacted on impulse.

The disturbing attack of his voice caused her to drop the pipe, which broke upon contact of the tiled floor.

"Damn it! What the fuck is wrong with you?" Mary said in a perturbed manner, while frantically scrambling for the small piece of dope.

He pointed down at the floor in front of the sink. "There it go right there."

Relieved, she picked the dope up and said, "Boy, you scared the living shit out of me. I wasn't even going to smoke it around you."

"My bad, I thought you forgot I don't like muthafuckas to smoke that shit around me."

Mary went into the backroom, returning five minutes later with an uneasy and restless personality. He knew she wasn't tripping off of the pipe being broke. All she was concerned with was finding the dope. She decreased the level of her normal tone to a whisper.

"Have you heard from LP?" she asked. "I've been paging his ass all fucking morning, but he won't call back."

Raekwon gave her a curious look. By that look, he was letting her know that he sensed there was an important reason why she wanted to get in touch with LP so bad.

"I ain't seen that nigga since yesterday. Why? What's up?"

"Well…I had been talking to him about something." She hesitated and stopped in the middle of her sentence.

Raekwon raised his eyebrows. Wanting to be nosey, he asked, "Talking to him about what?"

She hesitated for a minute and then said, "He'll probably get mad if I tell you, but I know you guys are tight and that you'll let him know. Well, the Colombian guys that my husband gets the marijuana from are going out of town tomorrow morning, and we have a key to their apartment."

Raekwon gave her a devious grin. "Oh yeah?"

She continued. "They don't know we have the key. We got it made the last time they went out of town."

Raekwon nodded to leave the impression that he caught on

to the scheme.

"We would be the last people that they would suspect to break in their house. We'll just tear up some shit so it won't look like we went directly to their stashes knowingly. We'll probably have to break out a window or two so it'll look like someone broke in."

"Where they live at?" Raekwon asked.

"Out in South Aurora." She sniffed and then wiped her nose with her forearm before continuing. "It'll be easy, but I'm not sure of how much smoke and stuff there'll be in there."

That was all that Raekwon needed to hear. It was on as far as he was concerned, and he was ready for whatever. He realized that he forgot to ask something, though.

"What time is we gonna go tomorrow?"

"Around seven or eight in the evening. I'll page the both of you."

The next night, he, LP, and Mary pulled into the alley and backed up on the opposite side the one-story apartments were on. They were in a car they had rented from a dopefiend. They all had on dark-colored hooded sweaters and gloves. It was a trip seeing a white female dopefiend dressed up like a criminal. Raekwon and LP laughed about Mary's appearance.

Raekwon was the getaway driver. So, he sat in the car with the engine running and crouched low in the seat. He was able to see over the dashboard, watching for anything suspicious from the neighbors.

He lifted up a blunt to take a puff and observed the apartments closely. Lights were coming on in different rooms, but there was no movement going on outside, which was good. It made everything go smoothly.

After fifteen minutes had passed, LP and Mary emerged from the darkness beyond the alley. They were each carrying a bag. Once they reached the car, they threw the bags in the backseat and hopped in. Raekwon pulled off calmly to ensure he didn't cause the neighbors to look out of their windows.

Upon arriving at Mary's house, they took the bags down into her filthy, unfinished basement, where they dumped everything out on her dusty pool table that had a two-by-four for one of the legs. There was only a half pound of weed and an ounce of cocaine. Those were the original items they went to get. Mary thought there might have been more dope and possibly some money in the safe that they couldn't get open.

Raekwon gave Mary a look of disappointment. "Safe? How come y'all ain't come get me to help y'all carry that muthafucka?"

"I started to get fucking paranoid," Mary replied. "I thought the neighbors might've heard me break the window while we were inside. We needed you out in the car anyway."

"Let's go back and get that muthafucka," Raekwon said, anxious to know what was in the safe.

"Hell no!" Mary shot back. "If we go back, we'll really look suspicious."

Among the other items in the bags were a few leather coats, a digital scale, a couple of handheld scales, several pairs of dress shoes, curtains, shirts, and some lampshades.

Raekwon sighed. "What the fuck we gonna do wit' them ugly-ass tap dancing shoes, them tight-ass pretty boy shirts, and shit for somebody's fuckin' house?"

By this point, Raekwon was on Mary's last nerve. She cut her eyes at him and said, "Stop fucking cussing at me. I don't cuss at you. All that other stuff is for me to sale. You don't have to have anything here if all you're going to do is complain."

"Aw yeah, I'm gonna get somethin' alright," he responded. "I didn't go to that muthafucka wit' y'all for my health."

"Y'all chill," LB interrupted. "We need to separate this shit."

Raekwon didn't know why he was tripping anyway. He should've already known that a dopefiend would grab some dopefiend items. The only thing that had him mad was the fact that the contents of the safe weren't included, if there were any.

Raekwon grabbed a leather jacket, a quarter pound of weed, and a quarter ounce of cocaine out of the whole deal. It wasn't much, but it was better than leaving empty handed. He had to hurry up and get out of that house before he ended up choking that dopefiend.

Raekwon and LP ended up at Kel's house after they left. Kel was sitting in the basement with Dre and Raylin, drinking and reminiscing.

Raekwon pulled out a bag full of weed and put a handful of it on the table. "Hey, Raylin, roll that shit up, nigga."

"Damn, nigga!" Raylin exclaimed. "Who you buy this shit from? Shit, we been tryin' to find some all day, but everybody's out."

Raekwon made eye contact with LP and then looked back at Raylin. "Shit, we just came up on this shit."

"Damn, y'all niggas got on leather coats and some mo' shit," Kel said.

Raekwon and LP just smiled without elaborating on the observation that Kel made.

LP sat down and picked up an empty bottle of beer. He stared at the bottle and shook his head. "Damn, y'all niggas been over here getting purved, huh?"

Kel sighed, looked towards Dre, and said, "Shit, we been chillin' wit' this crazy-ass nigga Dre all day. You know that nigga there is trigger happy. We was over there on March block hustlin', and this nigga Dre happened to see that dopefiend Leroy's van pullin' off from Poppa Randal's house. You know, the basehead you suspected of finding that dope you lost at the spot that day," he reflected, while explaining to LP.

"Yeah, yeah, I remember that shit," LP said, while nodding his head.

Kel continued. "This nigga pulled out his heat and started getting off on that fool. Ten minutes later, we ended up having to jump fences and shit all the way to Juan's house. Juan wasn't even there, so we couldn't get in the muthafucka."

"We coulda got in," Raylin interrupted, "but his bitch-ass sister was in there fuckin' some nigga or something. She wouldn't open up the door, so we just posted up in the backyard for about an hour. We kept hearin' police cars smashin' up and down the block lookin' for us, but we got away."

Raekwon laughed under his breath, gave a one-sided grin, and said, "Yeah, y'all know how that nigga is. He always—"

Dre cut him off. "Yeah, and I wish I woulda shot that skinless-ass muthafucka right in the back of his head. Don't act like y'all don't be getting us in all kinda shit, too."

"Yeah, we get in shit," Kel admitted, "but you be damn near getting a nigga killed or havin' a nigga have to kill a muthafucka over some bullshit and go to jail for somethin' stupid."

"Yeah, like when that nigga Dre cussed out some bitch up there at The Market," Raekwon added, "and some niggas jumped him over that shit. Remember that shit? He came and got us from over that nigga Pookie's house".

LP agreed. "Yeah, I was over there. We was coppin' some work from Pookie, and he even ended up strappin' up wit' us and hoppin' in his momma's Nova to help us look for them niggas. I had—"

Dre interrupted the conversation again. "Why y'all niggas all on me? Let my muthafuckin' nuts breathe. Shit." He changed the subject to divert things off of him. "I talked to that bitch Monica, and she said they was gonna be chillin' over at Vanessa and them's house."

"Who's all gonna be there?" Raekwon asked and then took a hit of the weed. With smoke coming out his mouth, he continued. "If Vanessa's big sister Tanji is over there, I ain't goin' 'cause that miserable bitch thinks she's somebody's momma. Y'all know she be on some bullshit."

Dre threw up his hands, unsure. "Shit, I don't know who's all gonna be over there with them broads, but I do know they said they got a gallon of Rossi."

Dre wasn't too much concerned with nothing but getting drunk, fucking with some broads, and running the streets. Raekwon was probably the same way, if he could see himself from the outside looking in. He didn't have enough wisdom to look at himself from that angle yet, but he was working on it.

Kel said he had a late-night hoodrat coming over, and LP didn't want to be around his cousin and her friends. Plus, his crazy-ass girl had been paging him all night.

When Raylin, Dre, and Raekwon approached Vanessa's

house on foot, they heard a lot of giggling coming from the backyard. There was a six-foot wooden fence surrounding the yard, so it was impossible to see what was going on. Raekwon handed Raylin the blunt and walked up to the fence. When Raekwon peeked through a crack in the fence, he saw Portia and Vanessa picking up one of their drunk-ass friends out of a pile of leaves. There was another girl sitting down, but her back was facing him so he couldn't see exactly who it was.

Portia was a sexy little chick that Raekwon had been trying to holler at for the past couple of months, but he wasn't really making progress with her because she was popping that Virgin Mary act on a nigga.

There was four broads in the backyard altogether. They hopped the fence and walked over to where they were chilling at.

Dre picked up the jug of wine off of the table and asked, "What the fuck is this?" He sat the bottle down and continued. "Y'all said it was a gallon over here, but this ain't no damn gallon. The shit ain't got nothing but a swallow left in it."

Vanessa stood up and walked over to the table. "I told my uncle to get a damn gallon, but he came back with this shit. I didn't really get to drink none of the shit because Monica's alcoholic ass drank most of it herself." She glanced over at Monica, who was sitting in a chair with her face buried in her arms on the table.

Drew reached in his pocket, threw a couple of dollars on the table, and asked, "Y'all wanna pitch in on two gallons of Rossi and some gin?"

When they got all of the money together, Raylin got on the phone and called up the street to his house. His brother Saul and one of his brother's friends showed up and drove to the liquor store for them. Raekwon was high, but he didn't really feel the little bit of liquor he drank over at Kel's house.

One hour later, there was Styrofoam cups everywhere, and they were all up in those female's ears. Raekwon was trying to holler at Portia,

"Trying hard to get some pussy, ain't you?" she said.

After she told him that, he was cool on her for the night. He didn't want her to get the wrong impression of him. He just backed off and sat back, sipping on his drink.

Vanessa got up and ran inside the house to answer the ringing phone. Looking through the window, Raekwon could see her. She hung right up. When it rang a second time, she did the same thing.

He went in the house, sat down at the kitchen table, and asked her, "Who you keep hanging up on?"

Before she could answer, the phone rang again. This time, she didn't answer it.

"That's just Felicia and Shamalika's asses callin' here drunk, talkin' all kinds of shit and yellin' in my ear tryin' to find out who's all over here."

"Where they at?" Raekwon asked, while reaching for the phone.

"They over some punk-ass nigga's house around the corner."

"Tell 'em to come kick it," he told her.

Fuck them," Vanessa replied with an angry tone. "They actin' stupid. Shamalika's drunken ass is gonna make me beat her ass if she calls me another bitch on the phone."

Raekwon wasn't really concerned with their personal beef;

he was more interested in trying to have a good time.

The phone rang again, and Raekwon answered it this time.

"Hello."

Shamalika's unmistakable voice replied, "Damn! Who's this wit' yo' sexy soundin' ass?"

"Stop playin', girl. You know who this is."

Raylin walked in the kitchen and asked Raekwon who he was talking to. He handed him the phone and told him to find out for himself. A couple minutes later, Raylin got off the phone with a one-sided grin.

"What them broads talking about?" Raekwon asked.

Vanessa looked at him and exclaimed, "Them drunk-ass bitches said they're on their way over here."

Felicia and Shamalika were some straight hoodrats. Everybody in The Maze knew they was some freaks. Raekwon knew quite a few niggas who were fucking with them bitches on the under. If you wanted to keep a good reputation with all the other broads in town, you would make sure they never found out you fucked either of them hoes.

After Shamalika and Felicia arrived, it started to get loud as a concert. Just like a bunch of ghetto hoodrats, they tried to drink up all of the liquor. Everybody was drunk and loud. Raekwon was surprised the neighbors hadn't called the police.

Dre pulled Raekwon and Raylin to the side and said, "Shit, Portia and them other broads is on some bullshit."

Raylin nodded his head in agreement with Dre. "Yeah, I was trying to holler at that stuck-up bitch Sasha, but she ain't talkin' 'bout shit. Ugly-ass Shamalika keeps tryin' to grab a nigga's ass. I don't know what type of shit she's on. I ain't trying to fuck wit' that bitch like that."

A couple minutes later, Raylin was trying to wrestle Shamalika's drunken ass away from him. She started flirting with all of them, pinching their cheeks and some more shit.

Felicia walked up and leaned on Raekwon's shoulder. Thinking she was trying to get affectionate with him, he damn near elbowed her in the chin. He had to make sure nobody else got the wrong impression.

He turned to Felicia and asked, "What the fuck are you doing?"

She gave him the 'fuck you, nigga' look and said, "Nigga, I was just trying to pass a message."

"Aw, my bad. What's up?"

Felicia got up in his ear and told him that Shamalika said she was going to fuck the shit out of Raylin if he even looked at her again. It was evident they wanted to kick it with them for the rest of the night. He could tell they were drunk and horny.

As soon as things started to speed up a little bit, Vanessa's miserable-ass older sister Tanji walked through the gate of the backyard. Raekwon could tell she was tired and angry by the look on her face. She worked at a fast food restaurant and always had to catch the bus to and from work.

Tanji stopped and twisted up her face. "Vanessa, what you doin' wit' all these niggas at Momma's house? You know she told you she don't want them over here no mo' after that time when they broke her vase. Yo' hard-headed ass just don't learn, do you?"

Vanessa spat back, "Who the fuck you think you is? You always in my muthafuckin' business about what I'm doin'. I was 'bout to leave anyway before Mom got home."

"Well, leave then, bitch!" Tanji responded sarcastically.

"Fuck you! I ain't the bitch, bitch!"

At that point, everybody in the backyard got up and headed for the gate to go to the front of the house, where they stood on the sidewalk. The mood was spoiled, and it was starting to get a little chilly outside.

Raekwon told Dre and Raylin what Felicia had told him about what Shamalika had been saying.

Raylin said, "I ain't fuckin' wit' that bitch."

"Nigga, you know that bitch wanna give all of us some pussy," Dre told him. "Carlos used to fuck that bitch in front of me all the time. I could've fucked her, too, but I never wanted to. I could settle for some of that low-budget twat tonight, though." He cleared his throat and continued. "When I was using the bathroom earlier, she walked in on a nigga and tried to grab my dick when I was puttin' my shit back in my boxers."

Raekwon looked at Dre. "Yeah, that broad is on some freaky-ass shit. She been flirtin' wit me, too. She keep on pinchin' on my cheeks and grindin' on my fuckin' leg. I ain't no fuckin' baby. That cheek shit was getting on my nerves."

"Nigga, stop complainin'. You know you liked that shit," Raylin said, teasing him. "Shit, fuck it. I'll fuck that bitch. Where we gonna take them hoes, 'cause we can't go to my crib?"

Raekwon quickly cut in. "We can't go to my house either 'cause my mom been on some bullshit today."

"Shit, we can go to my crib," Dre offered. "We gotta shake these other hoes, though. We gotta tell Felicia and Shamalika what's up, and then make Portia and them think we're all goin' our separate ways."

When they got to Dre's house, Raylin and Shamalika went

right in and down to the basement. Felicia stood outside on the sidewalk looking down the street for some reason. Raekwon had gone in the kitchen to grab a cup so he could pour him some Rossi.

Dre stood holding the screen door open. "Is you gonna come in or what?" he asked Felicia. "I ain't tryin' to wake my mom up so she can start trippin' on some bullshit."

"Hold up, nigga. I'm just waitin' for Sasha."

Raekwon was leaning against the counter in the kitchen, watching and listening to them while he sipped his drink.

"You either come in now, or you just ain't gonna get in." Dre started to get mad at that point.

When Felicia ignored him, he closed the door and locked it. Dre and Raekwon made their way down the stairs into his dark basement, where they heard some moaning coming from the back room.

Dre turned on the television and turned the volume down. Then they walked to the door of the room and looked in. As Raekwon's eyes adjusted, he noticed Shamalika was naked, bouncing up and down on top of Raylin over on the couch in the room. *Damn, this broad don't waste no time when it's time to fuck,* Raekwon thought.

Next, Raekwon and Dre walked in and pulled some chairs up in front of the couch so they could watch. Shamalika didn't even react to seeing them, and from what Raekwon had heard, it was all probably normal to her. He passed the bottle to Drew, who took a couple of swallows and then passed it to Raylin. Raylin started fucking Shamalika doggy-style and drinking at the same time.

Joining in, Drew started playing with one of Shamalika's

tittles, while Raekwon started caressing the other one. Her nipples were hard, and she was moaning just enough to make his dick get hard. This was nothing new, though; they had done this with plenty of freaks.

Shamalika finished off the last couple of swallows of Rossi. They had a thing about never drinking after broads like her, because they didn't know if the chick had just got finished sucking another man's dick or not.

Raylin flipped her on her back and started fucking her in the missionary position. It was getting kind of interesting, but Raekwon was about to get blue balls from the torture of playing with titties and watching Raylin get all of the pussy.

Dre broke the silence. "Damn, Raylin nigga, is you gonna share the pussy or what?"

"Hold up, nigga. I'm tryin' to bust a nut real quick. I—"

Raekwon cut him off. "Real quick? Nigga, you sweatin' and some mo' shit. You been up in the pussy for damn near thirty minutes. Nigga, you act like you tryin' to make love."

All of a sudden, Raylin's eyes widened. He hopped up as fast as lighting, looked down, and said, "Damn! My muthafuckin' condom broke." He then ran to the bathroom and turned on the light.

Shamalika's legs remained cocked open while Raekwon and Dre continued to play with her titties. Raekwon stood up and pulled a condom out of his back pocket. He had been holding on to it for so long that the package was cracked and all of the lubrication had nearly dried up.

He dropped his pants down to his knees, but kept his boxers on. He put the condom on and then played with Shamalika's clit so he could get fully aroused. He fucked her for a couple of minutes before he busted a nut and got up.

Raylin was standing in the back room, leaning on the dresser smoking a cigarette. Raekwon walked over to the dresser and picked up the cup of liquor he had set down earlier. He and Raylin whispered to each other while they watched Dre and Shamalika do the damn thang.

"What the fuck y'all niggas back there giggling and whispering like little bitches about?" Shamalika asked in a defensive manner.

"Who you callin' bitches? We ain't talking about yo' bitch ass anyway," Raylin responded, while turning on the light.

Shamalika told Dre to get the fuck up and then started gathering her clothes from all over the room. "Where's my panties at?" she asked.

Seeing the panties under a chair, Dre picked them up with his thumb and index finger as if he was picking up a snotty piece of tissue. He scrunched up his nose as he held them up in the air. "Here these nasty muthafuckas go right here. They got a doo-doo stain in 'em, too. Look."

Raekwon and Raylin started laughing and making comments about the panties. They were just some young dudes that didn't have any respect for a female that didn't respect herself.

Shamalika snatched her panties out of Dre's hand, cut her eyes at all of them, and said, "Fuck all y'all punk-ass niggas." She was in her feelings about how she was being bashed, and it was apparent from her demeanor. Behind those eyes of hers, Raekwon sensed a plot. She snatched the ponytail weave out of her head and stormed up the stairs.

"That bitch act like she don't know that the front door takes a key, and I got the muthafucka," Dre said.

"Come let me out this muthafucka!" Shamalika yelled down from the top of the stairs, seconds later.

Dre hurried to the stairway and snapped. "What the fuck you yellin' for? You gonna wake up my mom, and she gonna cuss yo' stupid ass out. I'm—.

Shamalika cut him off. "Nigga, I don't give a fuck what she does. Just let me out!"

***

The next morning, Raekwon, Raylin, and Dre woke up in juvenile hall with rape charges. Raekwon was hysterical. To him, Shamalika was every type of scandalous bitch that he could think of. He never would've thought he would be in such a situation.

After a couple of days passed, Raylin was released. It was easy for him to get his break from the situation because of how Shamalika let it be known to everybody at Vanessa's house that she was going to fuck the shit out of him. On the other hand, Dre and Raekwon were told it was their word against hers since there was nobody other than Raylin to coincide with the story they explained.

They fought the case for months to no avail. Trying to convince a jury of people whose ages were fifty and over that running trains were a normal occurrence in their day and age, and that Shamalika was a willing participant, was like trying to get the American people to vote for a black president during the days of segregation.

They ended up having to do a couple of years in the bing over something that didn't go down the way it was portrayed. Raekwon's whole strike in the game was messed up at this point. The little bit of respect he ever had for women of her caliber was now dead. His music career was temporarily put on hold, and his reputation was questionable.

There was more to learn from life. He had to recollect his thoughts and reevaluate the situations he was unintentionally getting himself caught up in.

As he sat back and reflected on the chain of events he failed to read as signs before he got himself caught up in a mouse trap, it revealed that there was a storm he had been carried through. He had escaped death on several occasions. The problem was he never took the time out to show he was thankful for it.

The Maze was a mess. Donnie had gotten locked up for an attempted murder, and Davon was sentenced to almost twenty years for the accidental murder of a child in a drive-by shooting where he didn't even pull the trigger. Dean, Darryl's brother, was on trial for a shooting that left one of the rivals dead. Darryl's homeboy, who was also involved, fled town and ended up getting robbed, tortured, killed, and stuffed in the trunk of his car. The rival gangs in town were killing each other off, one by one.

The further Raekwon had walked in life, the more confused he had become. It seemed as if he was going to have to learn everything the hard way.

THE BLEEDING PUDDLES OF GREED

CHAPTER 9

I t was a long and rough road getting adjusted to his new environment. Four months had passed, and Dre and Raekwon had caused four months' worth of problems already. They had somehow worked their way into the same pod with each other so the time would be a little easier to do. Dre had gotten into several fights with dudes over dumb stuff.

They were on some scandalous shit. They were hustling up on other dudes' canteen. They had to have their late-night candy bars to snack on, so they pulled a scam. They came up on some lightweight sandpaper looking shit, which they tore into small squares that looked like they could pass for acid. Raekwon was the late night orderly, so he had access to the clearing supplies, which they used to coat the paper with. He didn't know how it worked, but it did.

It was uncomfortable living with people who had different ways of doing and saying things. He knew it was time for him to capitalize, and to do that, he had to play on people's weaknesses.

The female staff escorted their pod over to the gym to play basketball. In the gym, there was a row of metal picnic tables that sat off to the side. They always kicked it at the last table that was the closest to the back wall. The white boys knew this, but they decided to post up at their table to play checkers and hacky sack.

Dre, Raekwon, and two other dudes who they chilled with assumed the white boys were trying to intentionally disrespect them. They all headed towards the table with poker faces.

There was a white boy named Andy, who had only been at the facility for two weeks. All the rest of the white boys latched onto him and followed closely behind whatever he did. Andy was a pretty big dude for his age. His characteristics let you know that he grew up around older dudes. He thought he was macho and he had a smart-ass mouth. Raekwon would always listen at how he talked to the guys that he hung around.

Raekwon walked up to Andy and said, "Hey, man, we sit at this table every time we come up in the gym."

"So what are you trying to say, dude?" Andy sarcastically responded.

Raekwon gritted his teeth. "We tryin' to get this table." He pointed at the next table over and continued. "Y'all can get that one right there."

One of the other white boys stood up and said, "They do sit here all the time, Andy. Let's just go over there."

They got up and took the hacky sack to the middle of the basketball court. Andy cut his eyes at them before walking off. Raekwon wanted to say something, but he just let it go.

They sat down and told war stories for a while. They were so animated and descriptive about their situations that it made Raekwon feel like he was right there in the story, watching everything go down.

A couple of dudes approached them and challenged them to a game of basketball. They agreed to play a game of four on four. One of the dudes from the other team went and approached Andy and his friends to try to give them a hard time. The staff lady noticed what was going on, and she cleared the court so they could run the game.

They hadn't been playing for more than five minutes before a plastic chair was thrown onto the court. When Raekwon looked towards the direction of the commotion, he noticed Andy standing there laughing with his friends as if he should be respected for what he had just done.

Raekwon's facial expression turned sour. He couldn't figure out what Andy was trying to prove. It just wasn't making any sense to him, but something had to be done about it. So, Raekwon dropped the basketball and headed towards Andy with fire in his eyes. Dre and the others followed right behind him as if it was a movement.

Raekwon stood face to face with Andy. "What the fuck type of—"

Before he had the chance to finish checking him, Andy had called him a nigger while simultaneously connecting his fist with Raekwon's chin. He was caught unexpectedly. Raekwon didn't see any of it coming, and he damn sure didn't think the white boy had the heart to step over that line.

Raekwon reacted off of instinct, snapping on him, and the dudes with him started throwing punches at every white boy in sight. He was diving from off of tables with elbows in the air and blindsiding Andy every chance he got. His mind blanked out, and all he thought about was attacking. Raekwon hit one of the dudes so hard, he fell to the floor. He bent over him and began to hammer away at his face. The white dude had his face covered with his hands, though, so it was hard for Raekwon to get at him like he wanted to.

"Watch out!" Dre yelled, as he came running from across the gym. He kicked the boy dead in the mouth, and blood squirted out of him like it was a sprinkler.

Raekwon jumped back to avoid getting any blood on him. "Damn, nigga! You done fucked that fool up."

A herd of staff rushed into the gym, anxious to subdue everyone who was involved in the matter. Raekwon tried to duck away into the crowd of onlookers and act as if he had no role in the scuffle. He wasn't the least bit surprised when the female staff pointed him out as a suspect. He was put in handcuffs and escorted out of the gym.

Everybody involved got sanctioned to thirty days of being locked up in their rooms. The room restriction wasn't so bad, though, because it gave Raekwon time to think and write lyrics.

On room restriction, he had a cellmate named Mario who was mixed with French and Puerto Rican. He was a real cool dude, but he had a short temper with the staff. He would always kick the door whenever he wanted to get the staff's attention. Mario was on room restriction for spitting in one of the staff's face.

Mario had an inside connection on cigarettes through one of the staff. Louis was a staff member who worked the graveyard shift. He was the only one on the staff that Mario got along with. Louis was cool, but Raekwon would've never suspected him of trusting someone like Mario.

It was a Saturday night, several days after Raekwon was first put on room restriction. He and Mario were playing tic-tac-toe on the cell wall. Sometimes they got so bored that they would make up stuff to do, like create their own games or tell scary stories just to pass the time.

Raekwon got up and looked out of the little window on the cell door, while Mario began kicking the door.

"Who's kickin' the damn door?" Lois yelled.

Mario yelled back through the door, "Room four! I gotta use the bathroom!"

Mario thought he was as slick as a can of oil, but Raekwon knew exactly what was going on. There weren't too many things a person could get passed him without him recognizing the motive behind it.

Fifteen minutes after Mario came back from the bathroom, Louis began to make his body-count rounds. He approached their room, shined the flashlight in on them, and slid a cigarette and a couple of Jolly Ranchers under the door.

Raekwon had never really been into cigarettes, but he sure wasn't going to pass it up. They created a spark from the light switch to light the cigarette. It was a trip how creative a person became in jail. He needed to relieve some stress, and that's exactly what he did.

Once he got off of room restriction and unclogged his disruptive state of mind, Raekwon began to see a lot of things in a different point of view. He realized there was a way of not compromising who he was as a person and to stop being a problem child. He was growing up and had to get a little more mature, and not cause any unnecessary attention while doing it.

Raekwon started to tighten up in a lot of different areas in his life. Every time he called home, which wasn't very often,

Roxanne would say, "Boy, you gettin' smart, and it seem like your spirit is so calm."

Kenny was a black staff member and the coolest of the whole facility. That was Raekwon's personal opinion. He was about six feet tall with a beer belly. He had a stripped out s-curl that he kept slicked back or pulled into a ponytail that wasn't even an inch long.

Kenny treated them like men instead of animals or children like most of the other staff treated them. Raekwon respected him for that. Kenny would always sit him down and have long talks with him about getting himself together in life so he'd have the opportunity to do the things he always wanted to do. He wasn't on all the black power propaganda, but sometimes he came real close to the edge.

Raekwon walked up to the staff desk where Kenny was sitting after the pod was locked down. He had just finished cleaning up his area as an orderly.

"Can I use the phone now?" Raekwon asked.

"Yeah," Kenny told him, "you can go ahead and use it, but only for a couple of minutes and only if you don't mind being seen on it by Ms. Hancock. You know she's here tonight working the control desk out there."

"Oh yeah," Raekwon said, remembering that Ms. Hancock was still in the facility.

They would always call her Fat-ass Bertha when her back was turned. She would never know who said it, so she would just be evil to everybody that was in the vicinity. She especially didn't like Raekwon and a couple of other dudes.

"She don't like me," Raekwon said, "and I don't like her either. So, I don't even want her to catch me on the phone since

I ain't really supposed to be on it anyway."

Kenny shook his head. "Y'all better leave that lady alone. Watch and see what I tell you. She gonna get one of y'all stacked up with incident reports to make it so whoever it is won't have a choice of making a decision as to where he might be transferred to as his permanent placement when he leaves here."

"She can do that?" Raekwon asked in disbelief.

"Yeah, that lady has a lot of pull around here, and she can basically do whatever she wants to do."

"Damn, that's crazy. These people can do whatever the fuck they wanna do. It's always something." Raekwon damn near growled the words out of his mouth, and then went on. "Urrgh, I hate this muthafuckin' place!" He then balled his fist up and swung his arm through the empty air in a frustrated way.

Sometimes, the simple fact that he was in juvenile jail would catch up with him and bite him in the ass. Some days, he would wake up and think to himself realistically. He was going through the motions, but that was just a part of life that was inevitable.

Kenny stroked his beard. "Have a seat." He leaned back in his chair and continued. "You're an intelligent young dude, you know. I would hate to see you get back out there and get killed or something for making the wrong decisions in life."

"Naw, not me," Raekwon responded, like he had all the answers he needed in life.

"Yeah, ok. I heard that one many times before and have seen the total opposite results. Some of y'all young brothas don't know the difference between right and left. You can't just run around here and fuck all your time by not tryin' to learn how to be responsible. What about when you have a child? Or do you already have any children?"

"Hell naw. I'm too young to be taking care of anybody's kids."

"Yeah, you're right, but I've seen a lot of young guys your age with children. They can't even take care of their children because they don't know how to take care of their damn self. You gotta think about your future all the time. Where do you see yourself in five years?"

Caught off guard, Raekwon gave him a dumbfounded look and said, "Shit, five years from now ain't promised to me. Ain't nothing promised." He shrugged his shoulders. "I don't know."

Kenny cut in before he could continue. "I ain't sayin' nothing is promised. I'm just sayin' you have to set goals in your life—long term and short term goals."

"I got goals, but you know, I grew up in a fucked-up environment. Ain't nobody ever mentioned being no doctor or lawyer or none of that shit in my neighborhood. Most of the white kids got good families and never had to experience welfare or witness they mom strung out on dope. My only hope is music or selling dope."

"Why can't you just do music instead of selling drugs, too?" Kenny shrugged his shoulders and locked them in that position. He was waiting for a response.

"I ain't saying I sell drugs, but that's the type of shit that goes on in my neighborhood. I used to see it go on every day." Raekwon didn't want to let him know that he sold drugs because when he really thought about it, he worked for the people who locked him up for some bullshit. The people who Raekwon hated so much. He kept himself humble about things that could've been incriminating because some people, no matter who they thought they really were, always found a way of helping things catch up to you and bring you down.

Raekwon ended up being very receptive to a lot of things that Kenny would sit down and talk to him about. They ended up getting real cool. He halfway understood some of the things that Raekwon was up against as a teenager that knew nothing more than the street life. He wanted to test just how cool he really was.

Raekwon's step-dad Ben came to visit him on a Sunday. He brought up a recorded CD that Tone had told him to give to Raekwon. The CD had a couple of songs that Raekwon had done and a couple of songs Tone had been working on with some of the dudes that he knew.

He and Ben talked for a while. All he really did was try to give some words of encouragement, let him know everything at the house was okay, and inform Raekwon that he wasn't missing out on anything. He let him know who he thought his real friends were and told him to make something positive out of this negative situation. He revealed to Raekwon that he knew he had been selling dope when he was out. Ben also told Raekwon that he had gone searching through his room and found an ounce of dope in the ceiling panels, but he was going to leave it where it was until he got home.

Raekwon wondered why Ben took the fact that he was selling dope so leniently. There had to be more to it. He thought he was going to bash him about it, but he didn't. He tried to play his role as a father figure, but Raekwon would never fully accept him as that, and he had his reasons.

The visit turned out to be nice. When it was over, Raekwon

explained the contents of the CD to Kenny and the reason why he wanted to keep it with him.

Kenny gave him a 'don't be trying to get over on me' look and said, "Let me take it home and listen to it first so I can check it out and see what you're working with. What songs are you on?"

"Numbers eight, thirteen, and fifteen." Raekwon was amped, answering with confidence.

Three days passed by, and when Kenny finally brought the CD back, he complimented him on his songs. He then told Raekwon that he could listen to it on the unit radio whenever he was there, but he would have to take it up in the laundry area and play it low.

This was the first step to getting what he wanted. It wasn't hard to get what he wanted when he was persistent about it. He started to be a little smarter about a lot of things just so they would work in his favor instead of against him.

Raekwon was finally transferred to permanent placement. Dre got shipped out of town away from his family because he couldn't seem to stay out of all the bullshit that was going on. He was just glad he got to stay in the state, even though it was still a great distance from where his family lived, which would limit his visits.

The place was pretty big. It was set up similar to a college campus. The only view Raekwon could see from there was the mountains and open fields. It was like being stuck in the middle of nowhere.

There were a couple of dudes there that he knew from the streets. One dude in particular that he got along with real cool was Lil' Madman. He was sentenced to juvenile life for murder.

He had always been wild. He never went to school and all he knew how to do was gangbang. He seemed to have matured just enough to keep himself off of room restriction.

Raekwon was in his cell sitting on the bed and reading a magazine. He was into the magazine because it was talking about the next generation of rap and how music was changing. He always kept up with the direction that music was going in and tried to learn more about the game.

Lil' Madman knocked on the door and walked in. "What you lookin' at over there, nigga?"

Raekwon lifted his head up and cleared his throat. "Just this lil' magazine about music. What's up wit' you, nigga?"

He pulled the chair out from the desk and sat down. Raekwon could tell he had something on his mind by the look of embarrassment that reflected off of his face. Lil' Madman pulled an envelope out of his pocket, pointed to the name it was addressed from, held it so Raekwon could see it, and asked, "Whose name that say right there?"

Raekwon looked at the name. "L. Paige. Why you ask me that?" he replied, giving him an awkward look.

"Aw, I didn't know who it was at first. I thought it said Pay-I-Gee. That's my Auntie Lisa, though, but she ain't never wrote me since I been in here."

"Nigga, you knew what that shit said. Why you playin'?"

Lil' Madman gave him a serious look as if he offended him and said, "Cuz, I can't read."

Raekwon never realized Lil' Madman couldn't read because his diction didn't show any weaknesses. He was tripped out when he began to reflect back to how he never received any mail and never read books or magazine. He always noticed the lady that used to come and grab him out of the unit to take him over to the education building every afternoon. He always thought she was just a math tutor or something, but now, Raekwon had put two and two together.

Raekwon looked at Lil' Madman in disbelief. "Damn, nigga, I ain't even know that shit."

Lil' Madman confirmed Raekwon's assumption. "Yeah, that's why that one bitch be coming to get me all the time. She be teachin' me how to read. I—"

Raekwon cut him off. "Why you referring to her as a bitch if she tryin' to help you out?"

"Shut up, fool!" he nonchalantly exclaimed.

Raekwon looked at him seriously. "Nigga, I'm for real. She seems like she gives a fuck about who you are."

"Well…that lady. You feel better now?" he replied sarcastically.

Through the months that passed by, Raekwon observed the sincerity of the lady that was helping Lil' Madman learn to read. He learned her name was Ms. Grenada, but she preferred to be called by her first name, Stacy.

Stacy looked to be in her early forties. There was a gentle spirit about her. Stacy was different from all of the other teachers and staff; a little more open and concerned. Raekwon came to know her personally, and they had good chemistry. He told her that he always read Lil Madman's mail to help him out. She didn't like to call him by his gang name, so she would call him by his first name, Calvin, which he resented.

Sometimes, Raekwon observed some of their sessions from afar to see why he would sometimes return to the unit mad. From Raekwon's observations, he noticed Lil' Madman would get mad at her whenever he couldn't pronounce certain words. He would just shut down and go for weeks without speaking to her.

Raekwon approached Stacy one day when she was sitting in her classroom by herself correcting papers. "How come Calvin won't speak to you? He won't tell me what's up."

"You know how he gets into his little shitty attitudes," Stacy said. "I told him that he won't ever learn how to read if he doesn't let me bring him the Hooked on Phonics program. He said I was trying to embarrass him. He got really on the defensive and called me a stupid Mexican bitch." She began to soften her speech, breaking down in tears before continuing. "He said I only cared about white people and that that's why I used to be married to a white man. I've never been racist towards anyone."

Raekwon had a long talk with Stacy, and told her that he knew Lil' Madman didn't mean anything he had said. He told her that part of the problem was that Lil' Madman had started developing feelings for her and didn't know how to express them because he didn't think she would accept him

Stacy looked dead at Raekwon. Her eyes were bloodshot red as she gave him a surprised look. "Are you serious?" she asked with doubt in her voice. "Well, that explains a whole lot. Why didn't he just tell me? It would've made things a lot easier to figure out."

There was silence.

Stacy sniffed, and with a stuffy nose, she asked, "Does anyone other than you know that Calvin has a crush on me?"

Raekwon gave her a serious look. "Hell naw. I'm the only person that he talks to about shit like that, and I would never even think about saying nothing about it to nobody. It ain't nobody's business." He had to stiffen up Lil Madman's image. "He's a real quiet dude about that type of shit, and I know him from the streets. So, I know he's a good muthafucka."

She was soaking it all in. He could tell she cared about him more than she had let him know. There was something about her that let Raekwon know she didn't want to bottle up her true feelings any longer.

Stacy bit her bottom lip and cut her eyes towards him. She thought for a while longer and then said, "Tell him to come talk to me."

Raekwon had never before seen an older woman with so much going for herself have such feelings and so much concern for a young black teenager who came from a corrupt backyard. That alone taught him about the sugarcoated, professional attitudes that some older women portrayed, when deep down inside, they were attracted to things that were against their so-called tradition.

Raekwon saw Lil' Madman back at the unit sitting at the card table by himself, thinking. Raekwon had a feeling that he was contemplating about Stacy, because that was the only time he was ever down and out.

Raekwon walked over to the table and sat down. "What's up, my nigga?" He was attempting to brighten up his mood.

Lil' Madman put his elbow on the table and rested one side of his face against his clutched fist. "Shit, just sitting here thinking and shit."

"I hollered at Stacy today, nigga."

There was suspense to that statement.

Lil' Madman sat up, gave him eye contact, and sighed as his

eyes wandered away in guilt. "Man, fuck her. I don't even wanna talk about her."

The way he responded wasn't enough to convince Raekwon that he didn't care. He knew that he was just being stubborn. He knew he really wanted to know what he talked to Stacy about.

"Look, nigga, that woman got feelings for you, homie. You need to let that stubborn shit go and get up under her to get what you want. I think she'll damn near do anything for you."

Lil' Madman became interested in what Raekwon was telling him. By now, Raekwon had his undivided attention. There was something about the way he expressed things to him that made him really listen to him and take him seriously.

"What did she say?" he asked nonchalantly.

"What you really wanna know is what I said. Nigga, I told her that you had a crush on her and—."

He cut me off angrily. "Nigga, why you do that shit?"

"Hold up, fool. Let me finish. I got this shit under control. She was crying over you and some more shit. You really hurt that broad's feelings."

"Why you callin' her a broad?" he asked sarcastically.

Raekwon spat back, "At least I ain't callin' her a bitch, though, but that's beside the point. Like I was sayin', homie, you all in wit' her. She asked me why you ain't tell her that you like her."

"Man, I love her," Lil' Madman admitted, with passion his voice.

"Well, whatever it is that you feel for her, nigga, you need to go holler at her, apologize, and all that good shit." Raekwon was trying to lace him and have him approach her in a mature way.

He damn near got hysterical. "Apologize? For what?"

"Nigga, just do it. You gotta understand that she's older, and she appreciates all that type of shit. You got to let her know in so many ways that you like her. You gonna have to grow up, homie."

From that point on, Lil' Madman started maturing whenever he dealt with Stacy. They started to get real close and all of their feelings were out in the open to each other. Nobody knew what was going on but the three of them. It was trip to see the strength of their love grow even though the circumstances were awkward in every way that one could imagine.

As time progressed, Raekwon progressed with it. The words his caseworker told him when he first got to the placement were repeating in his head like a broken record. She told him that if he successfully completed the level system of the facility, she would put in a referral for him to get six months of juvenile parole so he could get out early.

Raekwon finally decided to call home to check and see what everybody had been up to lately. It was hard to keep in touch when he only got to use the phone once a week for ten minutes.

"Hello."

"What's up, nigga?" Raekwon said.

"Shit, ain't been doin' nothin' but the same ole' shit," Tip replied. Although he sounded like he was just waking up with a hangover, he still sounded like he was glad to hear from his brother. "Ain't shit to do out here. You ain't missin' nothin'. Niggas been out here goin' crazy."

"What you mean niggas is goin crazy?" Raekwon asked in a concerned tone.

Tip was silent for a couple of seconds and then said, "You

know that nigga Nick went to jail for attempted murder."

Raekwon was shocked. "Damn. What the fuck happened?"

"Him and that nigga LP was at some basehead's house when the shit happened. I guess LP was trying to get some money that the basehead owed him, but the basehead didn't want to come outside and give him the money. They say some older swole-ass nigga that had just got out of the pen came outside talkin' shit."

Raekwon asked, "Who is that fool?"

"I guess he was the basehead's brother or some shit. When the nigga punched LP in the eye, Nick pulled out the heat and shot the fool in the face."

Raekwon gritted his teeth with anger. Things on the streets were falling to pieces, but there was nothing he could do about it. He thought to himself, *That's what that nigga gets for putting his muthafuckin' hands on his homeboy.*

"Damn, that shit there is crazy." Raekwon felt miserable inside. There was silence for a few seconds before Raekwon spoke again. "Hey, nigga, these people sweatin' me, so I gotta get off this phone. Shit, be careful out there, though, and tell niggas I said what's up."

Tip said, "Alright then," and the two hung up.

Raekwon spent the rest of his day dragging around. When people asked him what was wrong, he told them nothing. He lay in his bed thinking and sleeping for the whole day.

The months passed by pretty quickly. He was doing everything it took for him to stay off of the edge. There was a lot of instances that made him want to knock someone's teeth out, but it wasn't even worth it. Sometimes he was just so frustrated that nothing mattered. Raekwon managed to stay focused and see the big picture.

He ended up getting paroled. It was a blessing to finally see the struggle that he was going through come to an end. He couldn't even begin to explain the feeling that he experienced. He learned and accomplished a whole lot in juvenile hall, but it was finally time for Raekwon to go home.

CHAPTER 10

It was an honor to be able to look in a real mirror once again. Raekwon had uncontrollable happiness leaking through the pores of his body. It had only been a couple of days since he had been back on the streets, but he was already trying to get back on his feet.

A whole lot of things had changed since he had been gone. There were a lot of new faces around town, and it made him feel a little uncomfortable. He was seeing people that were straight up and down, square as a block of cheese, when he got locked up who were now walking around with their chests inflated like pigeons. In addition, a lot of females had gotten thicker and better looking. Deep in his heart, he was bias towards a lot of females, and especially towards hoodrats in general.

Big Vic pulled up halfway in his driveway with his trunk rattling like the lid of an overflowing pot on the stove. He was always known to have a nice knocking-ass car stereo system.

Raekwon exited the house with a one-sided smile on his face. He was happy to see Big Vic still doing what he do, but just a couple of years older now. He hopped in the passenger seat of his car and gave Big Vic a half hug.

"Damn, nigga, you got this muthafucka reekin' like straight indo."

"That's what it is, too," Big Vic replied, while reaching in the ashtray and pulling out a blunt that was still lit. "Here, wanna hit this muthafucka?"

"Hell naw, I don't wanna hit that shit. I gotta take them punk-ass piss tests. I can drink, though."

"Oh yeah? I'm 'bout to go to the liquor sto' then. What you want, fool?"

Raekwon patted his pockets, knowing they were empty. "Nigga, I ain't got no bread."

Big Vic looked at him like he was stupid. "Shut up, fool. I got that taken care of already. All you gotta do is drink wit' a nigga when I buy the shit."

Three hours later, Raekwon was pissy drunk. He couldn't handle his liquor. Everything was spinning like somebody sped up the earth's rotation.

He hopped up and damn near broke down the door trying to get through his room and into the bathroom, where he hugged the toilet like he was in love. Earl just couldn't pass him up. He came out of the bathroom feeling a little more focused after his unannounced meeting with the porcelain god.

As Carlos, Raylin, Big Vic, and Bodine came stomping down the stairs sounding like a thousand elephants, Raekwon met them at the bottom.

"Damn, y'all niggas is loud. Y'all heavy-footed-ass niggas better not wake up my mom 'cause she gonna put all of us out."

The presence of his friends made it feel like the days before he left. The only difference was that they all were now a couple of years older. He was at least glad none of his homies turned into dopefiends while he was gone.

Out of the blue, Raekwon busted out laughing, and the others looked at him like he was crazy. They looked around the basement to see if there was something they didn't notice.

"Damn, nigga, what the fuck is wrong wit' you?" Bovine asked. "That jail shit got you crazy now, huh?"

"Naw, nigga, I was just reminiscing about when me, Big Vic, and Kel went to these broads' house. Me and Vic drank up a fifth of them bitches' grandma's liquor, while Kel was upstairs wit' one of them hoes trying to get some pussy."

Vic laughed. "Yeah, I remember that crazy-ass night. That hoe told us not to fuck wit' her grandma's bar, but we told the bitch that her grandma wouldn't mind if we had a little bit of her Christian Brothers, since she was a Christian."

They continued reminiscing back to funnier times until Raekwon ended up falling asleep. He hadn't realized how tired he was. He was too busy trying to keep up with everybody else. He woke up the next morning in the same position he fell asleep in. He didn't know he had been sleeping that long until he saw the sun peeking through the basement window. Everybody had disappeared.

After a few weeks, Raekwon was back on his feet. He bought a bucket to get from point A to point B. His parole officer wasn't sweating him, and that was cool. One of his older partners, who had a record store, printed out fake check studs for him since he and the job thing weren't getting along at all.

When Raekwon pulled up to The Market to grab a couple of

items, he noticed a purplish Jetta parked a couple of cars over. The female inside the car looked a little familiar, but he couldn't quite make out who it was because she was facing the other way. As she was backing out, her face turned in his direction and he instantly identified the face.

"Hey, Faith!"

She immediately hit the brakes and made eye contact with him. She pulled the car up to where he was and cracked a big smile before getting out to give him a tight hug.

Faith was a redbone who had long silky hair, slightly slanted eyes, perfect titties, and full lips. Raekwon used to holler at her quite some time ago, but she wouldn't let him fuck. She was on that 'I'm a virgin and I'm not ready yet' shit back then.

He licked his lips like he was cool. "Damn, girl, you done got thick on a nigga, huh?"

Faith blushed. "Yeah, I done put on a little weight. I feel fat."

"Fat? Shit, you far from bein' fat. That's all ass right there."

"Shut up, boy." She looked as if she was reading his reaction and asked, "You know I had a son, right?"

Raekwon gave her a curious look. "Oh yeah? Naw, I ain't even know about that. Who yo' baby daddy?"

Faith sighed. "That sorry-ass nigga Melvin. I can't stand his ass. I'm glad I ain't wit' him no more, but that still don't stop his ass from being jealous."

By the sound of it, Raekwon sensed she was dealing with a lot more than she could handle. He knew who her baby's daddy was, but they never really spoke to each other. He figured if her baby's daddy didn't know they were kicking it, then he wouldn't have any problems out of him. And why would he anyway when they weren't together anyway? So, they ended up exchanging phone numbers, and Raekwon told her to keep in touch.

The next night, there was a record release party being thrown by a rapper named Suspect. Raekwon heard it was supposed to be the place where everybody was going to be.

He and LP pulled up to the event in a beige Caprice they had rented from a dopefiend. The event was being held in a hotel ballroom, and the parking lot was almost full. All Raekwon saw in the parking lot was gangbangers and hoodrats.

When they got inside, he saw a lot of his homies sitting at the tables by the bar. There were crews of dudes and females all in their own sections of the room. He had noticed two rival gangs from the area. Since nobody was tripping, he paid it no mind.

Raekwon sat at the bar and had a couple of drinks. He saw a lot of people he hadn't seen in a while. Damn near all of the dudes he knew were there. He saw Elgin, Black Eddy, Cary, Kel, Carlos, Big Vic, Bodine, and Dre. Elgin and Cary were on the microphone freestyling and making everybody laugh.

"Damn, that bitch's ass is eatin' a hole in them pants!" Black Eddy said, loud enough so the female that he was referring to could hear.

"Nigga, who you calling a bitch?" She had beef in her voice, and it sounded like she was confident enough to knock him out for his comment.

Black Ed gave her a one-sided grin and sarcastically said, "Aw, my bad, hoe. I was just trying to compliment yo' stuck-up ass."

"Yeah, whatever, you dirty-dick-ass nigga." She walked off after rolling her eyes.

After about an hour of everybody getting full of drinks, the scene started to change. At first, there were chicks on the dance floor, but that floor slowly turned into a gang-sign-throwing gangsta boogie. There was a gap in-between the two gangs. No words or direct disrespect was being aggressed, but everybody couldn't help but observe. You could feel the tension floating in the air with the smoke.

The host, Suspect, got on the stage and announced that he was going to start the performances early. Raekwon knew it was just an attempt to ease the tension that was rising.

"Yeah, what's up, y'all?" Suspect said into the mic. "This song I'm 'bout to do is off my upcoming album."

As soon as Suspect started his song, a chair flew in the air and fights broke out in the middle of the dance area. There were some chicks jumping on each other and pulling weaves out. Even a couple of the dudes got knocked out.

The police had been circling the parking lot the whole night, so they weren't far away. A couple of minutes later, there was mace being sprayed in the ballroom by the police. Everybody was rushing the door and covering their faces with their coats and shirts.

Nobody got seriously hurt, but a couple of people left with beer bottle injuries and shattered car windows from the shootout in the parking lot.

A month later, Raekwon finally started to chill with Faith. She was cool and had some good conversation. He wasn't even focused on trying to sex her because she was good company and he didn't want to spoil that. He decided just to let nature take its course.

His phone rang, and he picked it up after two rings.

"Hello."

"What's up, boy?" Faith asked, trying to sound sexy.

"Boy? Girl, I'm a man. Get it right," he said jokingly. "But fuck all that. You soundin' sexy than a muthafucka. I bet you smellin' sexy, too, huh?

"Why you wanna know?" she teased.

"Shit, you took damn near an hour to hit a nigga back. I paged you a while ago. Twice." Raekwon stressed the last word and continued. "You musta been gettin' nice and fresh, huh?"

"Well, yeah, I did get dressed. But the reason it took so long to call back was because my son's father came to pick him up and didn't want to leave at first. So, I'm on my way to pick you up right now. Okay?"

"Oh yeah? Where we goin'?" he asked in surprise.

She was quiet as if she was thinking, and then replied, "Umm, I think I want to take you to the mall and buy you something. I saw something the other day that I would like to see you in."

He acted nonchalant, but he wanted to jump through the ceiling. *I got her right where I want her,* he thought to himself.

He smiled into the phone. "I ain't even gonna ask what it is because I know you ain't gonna tell a nigga. So, I'll just be here waitin' for you when you get here."

"Be outside waiting 'cause I ain't tryin' to be sittin' out in front of yo' house all day."

They hung up.

"I'm a muthafuckin' Mac," he whispered to himself with confidence.

He thought he had it made. He was finally experiencing the maturity of a girl that was growing into a woman. One who wanted to treat him like the man that he was becoming. Faith was only a year older than he, but she acted much older than her age. Having children does that to a lot of women.

He was standing in the living room when Faith pulled up across the street. He walked out to the car and greeted her through the driver's side window.

"What you waitin' for?" Faith asked. "Get in so we can leave."

Just then, Raekwon remembered he had a dope sack in his pocket. "Aw shit! Hold up. I forgot to grab somethin' real quick."

"Well, hurry up. I'm gonna go in the trunk and put a different CD in my CD changer. You better be back out here by the time I finish," she told him with a smile.

He returned her smile and said, "You're a demanding little pussycat, ain't you?"

She gave a soft laugh, and he ran in the house to stash the sack. He came back out, hopped in the car, and they pulled off.

He grabbed the remote control to her high-end stereo system and sarcastically said, "Damn, girl, you doin' it, ain't you?"

"No, you're the one doin' it. I remember all that money you used to have before you went to jail. You was sellin' weed in school and havin' it yo' way. I had to work hard, slavin' everyday just to keep up on my car notes. As a matter of fact, I'm late on one right now, and I'm glad I brought it up 'cause I forgot to put it in the mail. You don't mind if I stop by the post office real quick, do you?"

"Naw, that's cool wit' me," he replied, while changing through the music, trying to find something to listen to.

He relaxed and let the seat back. As they turned onto the block, he heard a loud engine and looked at Faith. "You hear somethin'?"

She lifted her eyebrows with curiosity. "Nuh uh. What you hear?" She snuck a glance into her driver's side mirror.

The engine of another car sounded like somebody was accelerating and then letting off the gas.

"Oh shit!" Faith screamed. She was panicking, and her face looked like she had seen a ghost.

Raekwon lifted his seat up so he could look over his shoulder and out the back windshield. He had been hit by shock. "What the fuck…" He couldn't believe what he was seeing.

Melvin sped up and drove next to Faith's car on the driver's side. He pointed at her, and through the rolled-up windows, his lips mouthed, "I'ma fuck you up, bitch."

Raekwon was angry. "Damn, you got this muthafucka right here. Let me out."

"No, no, no! He's gonna try to fight you." She started crying. "I'm sorry. I didn't know."

Raekwon wasn't trying to hear none of anything she was saying. He gave her a cold stare. "Stop this muthafuckin' car right here!" he yelled with his teeth gritted together to let her know he was serious.

When Faith stopped the car just short of the corner, Raekwon hopped out and stood on the sidewalk. Melvin parked sideways in the street right in front of her car to make sure she couldn't pull off.

Melvin jumped out of his car. He had Raekwon by about a hundred and twenty pounds and six years in age. Faith froze in her seat as he approached her car with rage in his eyes. She tried to reach over to the passenger side to lock the door, but he got to it before her.

Melvin snatched her keys out of the car, unlocked the driver door, and pushed her out. "Bitch, you tryin' to play me like I'm a muthafuckin' fool?" He got out and ran around the car.

Faith got up and stood in the street with her arms folded, answering his question with nothing more than cries.

Melvin got loud with her. "You think I'm playin' wit yo' stupid ass, huh? Bitch, fuck you!" He rushed to her car and sat down in the driver's seat. He snatched her stereo out of the dashboard and slammed it down in the street. Then he popped her trunk open, threw everything out of it, yanked her CD changer out, and slung it to the ground with brutal force.

He tossed her keys in the air and looked at Raekwon. Raekwon wasn't going to let his big ass get a hand on him, but he wasn't going to run either. He couldn't let him embarrass him in front of all the people who were standing outside watching.

Faith ran up to Melvin, yelling and pulling on his shirt.

"Don't hold that nigga," Raekwon said, while stepping up in the yard of the house on the corner.

Melvin came walking towards him, breathing like he had emphysema. "What the fuck is up, nigga? So you been fuckin' wit my girl, huh?"

Raekwon snapped back, "Nigga, fuck you! That bitch told me that y'all wasn't fuckin' around anymore." By now, Raekwon was backing up so he couldn't grab him.

156

"Well, she lied. Now, nigga, what's up?"

Raekwon could see the blind fury in his eyes.

Out of nowhere, he got an adrenaline rush and posted up with his knuckles up. "What the fuck is up then, nigga?"

Melvin's tried to rush Raekwon. He swung and grazed Raekwon's chin, but he slipped. As he was falling, Raekwon capitalized and gave him two to his jaw and face. When he fell, Raekwon kicked him a couple of times. Raekwon heard the neighbors in the background cheering him on since most of them knew him.

When Raekwon backed off, Melvin got up and went towards his car with a smirk on his face. He started walking down the street backwards.

"Oh, so what? You gonna go grab a pistol and try to kill a nigga over a bitch?" Raekwon said.

Melvin didn't respond.

Raekwon turned around and started walking at a quickened pace while looking over his shoulders. Melvin started up his car and came his way. He smashed down on the pedal and swerved towards Raekwon, chasing him into somebody's front yard. He hit their trash can and knocked it into the air.

Raekwon grabbed a handful of rocks, ran into the middle of the street, and threw them at his car with all of his might. Melvin hung out of the window and glanced back for a split second while flipping him off. The good thing was that he didn't turn around.

Raekwon had rage throughout his whole body. He jogged to Big Vic and Isaac's house, which was only around the corner. After he told them what happened, they strapped up and went looking for Melvin, but he was nowhere in the hood.

After Raekwon finally calmed down, he decided to let the issue go because he came out on top. He knew if Melvin would've been able to get a hand on him, things would've ended up a whole lot different.

CHAPTER 11

It was a full moon when Raekwon pulled up in the parking lot of the Sierra Vistas. They were some low-income apartments for single mothers. They also served as a front for dope spots and a way to beat the system out of money, but most of the tenants had legit housing needs.

A lot of hoodrats he knew lived there so he was glad it was nighttime so they couldn't see him creeping. Most of the broads that lived in the building always had something to gossip about. He had arrived at gossip central, so he had to be careful.

Raekwon turned off his headlights, backed into a parking space, and got on his cell phone. After three rings, there was an answer.

"Hello," a soft voice answered.

He licked his lips as if he was face to face with the person on the other end of the phone.

With a gentle tone, he said, "What's happenin' wit' you, baby girl? I'm out here sittin' in the parking lot."

Shae smacked her lips, and in a sassy manner, she replied, "Nigga, don't be tryin' to pull that sweet shit. What took yo' ass so long anyway?"

Shae was really humorous and sexy when she tried to get smart. She turned him on even more when she acted that way. She made him think back to the time when he first met her several years ago. She still had quite a bit of that southern accent when she talked. She'd had a baby since then and got a little thicker, too. She always had an innocent look in her eyes, but she was scandalous.

Shae was a beast when it came to fake checks and burning up somebody else's credit card. That's how she got everything in her apartment. Raekwon didn't blame her for it because sometimes females had to get out and hustle just like dudes.

He let out a chuckle. "Shit, I had to stop by the liquor sto' and grab that Gin & Juice for you so I can toss that juicy ass all over the bed."

"Oh, is that right? Nigga, you ain't funny, but thank you for grabbin' that shit for a bitch. Is you gonna hurry up and come in or what?"

"Yeah, I was just makin' sure everything was still cool. I'm 'bout to come up in there right now."

She caught Raekwon before he hung up. "Hey, make sure you knock soft 'cause my neighbors is nosey and they always be up in my business. I'll hear you 'cause I'm sittin' in the living room."

They hung up.

Raekwon put his pistol under the seat, made sure his condoms were in his back pocket, grabbed the liquor out of the back seat, and got out the car.

When he got inside of her apartment, he sat down on the couch. He noticed Shae had incense and candles lit.

"Damn, girl. I see you tryin' to set the mood and shit."

She tried to keep a straight face. "Set the mood for what? I always light my incense and candles. It helps me go to sleep at night."

She must have thought he was a fool or something by the way she shot him that transparent response. He knew when a chick was trying to throw him the pussy, and this was one of those times. Shae was a sneaky one. She knew how to keep her name out of the streets, and that's one of the reasons he wanted to see how freaky she really was.

He popped back, "It sho' don't look like you tryin' to go to sleep to me. Fuck all that other shit you talkin' about. I would really appreciate it if you grabbed a nigga a cup of ice so I can cool off this Henn."

"Ewww, I don't see how y'all niggas drink that shit. That stuff don't taste right at all to me," she exclaimed while walking to the kitchen area to grab some cups.

When she returned, she sat real close to him in the dimmed living room. After they had a couple of drinks, there was some sexual vibes floating in the air.

Shae looked Raekwon dead in the eyes and asked, "You gonna spend the night, ain't you?

In a joking manner, he replied, "As long as you don't try to say a nigga raped you or nothing."

She giggled. "Shut up, nigga. I ain't that type of bitch. You know I ain't nothin' like that bitch that did that shit to y'all."

Everything was a gamble and he knew to be extra cautious, though.

When she reached for his dick, he grabbed her hand.

"Girl, what you doin'?"

"I'm tryin' to see what you workin' wit'."

He gave her a one-sided smile. "You'll see when I put yo' head through that wall when I'm hittin' it from the back. Hey, uh...where yo' son at?" he asked all of a sudden.

"Oh, he outta town wit' his daddy. I'm glad that trifflin'-ass nigga finally came and did somethin' wit' his son."

Raekwon felt relieved to know he wasn't going to have to get into it with another female's baby daddy. It seemed like almost every broad he knew with a child had something bad to say about the dude she had the child by. They loved the baby, but often regretted the baby's daddy.

Raekwon sat on the edge of the bed in the dark room, waiting for his eyes to adjust. He was fucked up, and he knew she was fucked up, too. After picking up some clothes from off the floor and stacking them on her dresser, she changed into a t-shirt with nothing else on underneath it.

While walking over to Raekwon, she asked in a sexy voice, "Ain't you gonna at least take off yo' shoes and yo' coat?" She then sat on the bed and laid back.

After removing his coat and shoes, he laid back in the bed next to her. She crawled up on top of him, lifted up his shirt, and started kissing and sucking on his chest. She then moved up towards his face and tried to kiss him. When he turned his head away, she got the point. He wasn't the kissing type, and he wasn't trying to make love to her.

"Hold up," Raekwon said, as he got up to take off his pants. He put them right next to the bed so he could reach in his pocket to grab a condom when he needed it.

He started sucking on Shae's titties, which caused her to get so aroused that she started grinding against his leg. He reached down and started to squeeze her ass cheek. Her wet pussy was dripping on to his leg, just calling him to come and get it. He was stalling the process on purpose to make her want him even more.

She turned on her back and he started finger banging her. Her moans were so soft and sexy that his dick immediately stood at attention. Her pussy was wet and tight, just the way he liked it.

She got up and told Raekwon to lie on his back. She then pulled his dick out of his boxers and started stroking him like a champ.

"Why don't you go 'head and just suck it?" Raekwon asked with a pleasant voice, as if trying to convince her it was the right thing to do.

"I'm sorry, but I don't suck no dicks. You gonna have to get one of them other bitches to do that for you," Shae sarcastically replied.

"Shit, don't kill a nigga for tryin'. I ain't said nothin' wrong by tryin' to get a little head."

Ignoring his comment, she tried to get on top of him.

"What is you doin'?" Raekwon said, putting his hand up to her chest to stop her.

"Just let me feel you."

Raekwon gave her a crazy look and said, "Uhn uhn. Hold up and let a nigga grab this condom real quick."

He rolled over and reached in his pants to grab a condom. When he turned back over, she tried to get on top of him again. This time, he wrestled her off of him and covered his dick with both hands. He looked at her like she was foolish. She was turning him off with her aggressiveness. He had never experienced anything like that before, and he wasn't going to let her play him like a sucker.

Raekwon angrily slurred, "What type of shit is you on?"

She tried to control him with those innocent eyes. "I just don't like condoms 'cause they irritate me."

"Shit, you just gonna have to be irritated or I'm gonna have to bounce 'cause I ain't wit' that bareback shit."

He thought to himself, *This bitch tryin' to stick me with a kid 'cause she know a nigga been out there tryin' to get a little money.*

He acted as if all the funny business never took place. He put on his condom and fucked the shit out of her. Afterwards, they both ended up falling to sleep, drunk and burned out.

Raekwon woke up at around three o'clock in the morning. He was mad at himself that he was still there. Shae had her arms wrapped around him like he was her man, and he wasn't cool with that at all.

He got up, put on his clothes, and went to the bathroom, where he checked his pockets to make sure all his money was there. He wasn't missing a dime. He was glad he woke up before her, because she was the type he would suspect to do some scandalous shit.

Later on that evening, he woke up at home trying to recover from his hangover. He had to get up and call Tone so he could cop some work. His pager had been blowing up so much that by the time he finally looked at it, it was full.

Raekwon got up off the basement couch and paged Tone. Then he went outside and sat on the front porch to get some oxygen to his brain. It felt like a clamp was tightening up on his temples. He closed his eyes and took a couple of deep breaths.

As usual, he began observing the activity on the block. It was like second nature for a hustler to be aware of his surroundings. It was something that had to been done at all times in order to stay on his toes.

He noticed a dark blue Lumina sitting at the corner of the block. There was a white man with shades sitting in the car with some reading material in his hands, but Raekwon couldn't see what it was that he had.

His heart dropped. He knew it was an undercover because this wasn't the first time he had seen that car in town. He also noticed a small antenna that rose out of the back windshield.

It wasn't unusual to see this in his neighborhood. The only unusual thing about it was seeing them parked on his block. There were only a handful of residents on that block, so the main thing was trying to figure out who they were after.

Raekwon watched the car out of his peripheral so it wouldn't be obvious that he noticed there was something suspicious going on. He'd begun to calm down because if it was him that they were watching, he didn't have any dope for them to find. He had a digital scale in the closet with some fishing equipment as the front for it. His pistol was in the car, and the car was in his mother's name. And there was no way they could've had a search warrant on her unless they were trying to play dirty.

The undercover pulled off from the corner and turned on the street right in front of his house. He didn't look Raekwon's way, but Raekwon did notice that he stared down the street for quite a while until he turned. Raekwon couldn't make out whose house he was looking at or if he was just looking at all of the little bad-ass kids that were playing in the street.

As soon as the Lumina disappeared, a squad van raced from around the corner and onto the block. The van sped over the speed bump recklessly. Unmarked cars were rushing in from every direction. The undercover cops pulled up in front of Raylin's house, hopped out the cars, and busted through his front door.

Raekwon thought about how sloppy Raylin and his older brother Saul had started getting lately by letting dopefiends come into their mother's house to buy dope. There was one dopefiend in particular that Raekwon didn't trust, but Raylin didn't want to listen. They called him Milk Man because he used to steal milk out of the boxes that got delivered to people's houses early in the morning. He would always ride around town on his mountain bike trying to trade the milk for crack.

There was a rumor going around about Milk Man, but Raekwon didn't know if it was true or not. A couple of people were saying he was responsible for getting some dudes busted up in the Crossing Apartments.

Raekwon didn't have to worry about the dopefiends getting him caught up in a raw deal because he had graduated from curb-serving and had started supplying the hustlers on a low scale. He was pushing quarters, halves, and ounces.

When the phone rang, Raekwon ran in the house and into the kitchen to answer it.

"Hello." He was breathing hard.

"What's up, nigga?" Tone asked. "What's wrong wit' you fool?"

"Aw shit, nothing. I just had to run in the house to catch the phone." Raekwon caught his breath, and the tone of his voice became serious. "Nigga, guess what?"

"What's up?" Tone asked curiously.

"I was spooked than a muthafucka just a minute ago. I was sittin' outside on the porch and all kinds of unmarked cars and shit went and ran up in Raylin's crib."

In a high pitched voice, Tone replied, "Oh yeah?"

"Yeah, that shit was too close to home."

"Uh huh. I remember you tellin' me that them niggas was down there being sloppy. What's up wit' you, though?"

"Nigga, I been tryin' to catch up wit' yo' ass for two days."

"Shit, I just got back in town. I was in Atlanta, and that shit was off the hook. Aye doe."

"What's up?"

Tone paused for a second and then said, "Come around to the crib like seven."

He knew exactly what that meant. It was back on. It was time for him to go cop some work and get back at the grind. The incident that happened at Raylin's house wasn't going to stop him from getting his money. It just hit so close to home that he had to be more cautious about the people that he was dealing with. Dopefiends weren't the only ones setting niggas up.

***

It was just getting dark when Raekwon pulled up to Tone's house. There was a maroon Impala on all gold Dayton's parked in front of the house. It looked like it was fresh out the paint shop by the way he could see the reflection of his car.

Raekwon parked, got out, and walked up to Tone's front door. Tone looked out of the little window on the door before letting him in. The whole living room reeked of marijuana. Tone and Mondo were getting high and drinking on a fifth of Hennessy.

Mondo was one of Tone's homies. Raekwon didn't really know Mondo that well, but every time he was around him, he got a bad vibe from him. Mondo had to be at least fifteen years older than Raekwon. He was cocky and very arrogant. For some reason, it always seemed like he was trying to get over on somebody in some kind of way, like he was trying to take advantage of somebody. Raekwon could see his sneaky side when he looked in his eyes.

After the Hennessy was gone, Mondo got up and left. Raekwon looked out the window when he was pulling off and saw it was his car that had been sitting outside.

"It's somethin' about that nigga Mondo that don't sit good wit' me," Raekwon said to Tone.

Tone gave Raekwon a curious look. "What you mean?"

"He just seem sneaky or something."

Tone softened up the look on his face and nonchalantly replied, "Aw, I know what you talkin' 'bout. I used to think that same shit about the nigga when I first met him, but he's cool."

Tone was pretty good at reading people, so Raekwon took his word for it. He just sometimes got uncomfortable around people who were out of the normal crowd that he was used to. That's probably where his concerns came from, but then again, his first instinct had a good reputation of being the truth.

"What you tryin' to grab?" Tone asked.

Raekwon thought for a second, then pulled out his money and started counting it. "Go 'head and shoot a nigga three of 'em."

"Shit, just shoot me the bread 'cause I'm 'bout to go grab this shit from my people right now. They been havin' a nigga waitin' all day 'cause they regular connect is out of town. They gotta get the shit from this other fool. I want to get the shit straight from dude my damn self, so I told them to have him meet me over there. You can shoot out there wit' a nigga if you want to. I just didn't want to have you in the car wit' me wit' all the dope while yo' ass is on parole."

Raekwon looked at Tone with a look that let him know that he didn't care. "Fuck that parole shit, nigga. I'm mobbin' up there wit' you."

Raekwon was a little tipsy during the ride there. The highway drive had him in a daze. Tone had Sugar Free's album, *Street Gospel*, bumping as he settled into his thoughts. This was the first time Tone had taken him on this type of mission with him. It let Raekwon know that times were changing, and that Tone trusted him in some way.

Sometime after they got off the highway and started driving down a side road, Tone turned the music down as they passed by a cemetery.

Tone stared at the cemetery and said, "Nigga, I trip off of cemeteries every time I pass 'em when I'm high or drunk."

Raekwon gave him an awkward look. "Why?"

There was a brief silence.

Tone said. "It just makes me think about how a nigga out here living, you know," Tone replied. "Tomorrow ain't promised, and a nigga got enemies. So many niggas is out here dyin', and I just gotta be real wit' myself by knowin' I ain't livin' no better than they was livin', you know?" He sighed and continued. "You gotta be on yo' toes, nigga, 'cause I be checkin' you out, and you a smart, young nigga. It seems like with each generation that hits the streets, the young niggas get wiser and wiser. This shit is bigger than rap. Niggas is really out here hustlin' to eat. You gotta realize that ain't no money like ya' money, but ain't no time like ya' time."

He really caught Raekwon's attention when he said that. Raekwon always had the right idea, but never thought of it in the way that Tone told him. What he was saying was real, and it was enough to get Raekwon more on point. Tone helped him get on his feet when nobody else would, and he had that much more respect for him because of that. He was like his other big brother.

Raekwon gave him the indication that he was feeling what he was saying to him. "Yeah, you right," Raekwon responded, while nodding.

"Lil' nigga, I got love for you and I don't wanna see nothin' happen to you. Always stay true to yourself and let them other niggas do what they do. You know, ain't no telling when them people gonna come for a nigga when you in the game, and a nigga can't go out like no mark."

"I feel you, my nigga," Raekwon said. "I grew up around this shit all my life. This is all I know, and I know about the consequences. I gotta stay ready for whatever."

The mood changed when Tone's cell phone rang. He answered the phone and had a brief conversation. Raekwon assumed the person that he was talking to was the person that they were going to meet. He told the dude that he was around the corner and was about to pull up in five minutes.

As they pulled up, Tone turned off the headlights on the car. He then told Raekwon to open the glove compartment and hand him the .45 semi-automatic that was inside. He laid the gun on his lap, reached in his pocket, and pulled out an envelope that was full of cash.

Tone handed him the envelope and said. "Here, hold this paper. It's like ten-five in there."

"A'ight." Raekwon grabbed the money and stuffed it in his left pocket.

Tone looked across the street to where a fat Mexican dude was standing outside the doorway of a dilapidated apartment building. The Mexican guy raised his hands up to catch Tone's attention.

Tone rolled the window down and said, "Hold up. Here I come." He then rolled up the window, looked at Raekwon, and said, "Here, just give me the money and you hold the pistol. It's already loaded wit' one in the chamber. So, all you gotta do is take it off safety if some shit gets funny. I don't trust this muthafucka. He don't think I know he just a middle man, but I'm 'bout to cut straight into his people right now."

They got out of the car and walked across the street to the apartments where the corpulent Mexican guy stood. He pulled Tone to the side, where they began an isolated conversation. Raekwon felt out of bounds. Anything could've happened at that point, like some kind of ambush or undercover police operation.

A silver Yukon turned out its lights as it slowed down and came to a complete stop in front of the apartment building. Raekwon put his right hand close to the .45 that was on his waist, trying to be sure not to make it look obvious. He was a little uneasy with all of the activity going on while they were trying to make a drug deal.

There were four Mexican guys in the Yukon. All of them got out of the truck except for the driver.

"There goes Marcos now," said the big fella that Tone was talking to.

Raekwon immediately gathered that the short one with the bald head was Marcos by the way the others posed as some type of bodyguards. It was a trip just watching how cautious and organized they seemed to be. Raekwon relaxed a bit after noticing the easiness to Tone's expression.

Tone told Raekwon to wait in the car and that he was going to be right back. Marcos signaled one of the guys that were with him with a nod as he walked into the building with Tone and the other two guys. The other guy then walked back to the truck. As Raekwon sat in the car, he observed the guy walking from the truck and back into the building with a dark duffle bag.

Fifteen minutes later, Tone exited the building with his coat balled up in his hand as if something was wrapped in it. He hopped in the car, and they left.

From that day forward, Raekwon began to raise his standards and make more moves than he was making before. His eyes had been opened a little bit wider to the game. He had to get on his feet, but most importantly, he had to hustle with patience. It seemed hard for him to get his money right because he was spending so much of it with high standards he had set for himself. He was on the edge of living beyond his means.

Raekwon got off of juvenile parole and started hanging tough. He was spending a lot of money on weed, clothes, liquor, and a whole lot of other stuff that he didn't need. It started to seem like there was a party in his basement every night.

Things started to fall apart right before his eyes. Roxanne moved out of the house and got her own apartment. She said that she couldn't accept what was going on in the house anymore. She told him that his step-dad, Ben, had been selling dope for years, which explained to Raekwon why Ben didn't trip with him the time he came to visit Raekwon in juvenile hall and told him that he found some dope of his that was stashed in his room. At that point, nothing surprised him.

Dudes that he had grew up with started telling him that he was being distant and acting like he wasn't trying to associate with them anymore. That wasn't the case at all. If anything, he was just doing too much and needed to focus, but Raekwon felt if he let his guard down now, it could be his downfall.

CHAPTER 12

Raekwon woke up and lay on the bed, staring at the ceiling. He was tired. Thoughts raced through his mind like lightning. He felt depressed, but had no understanding of how he could be depressed. It might've been his body telling him that he hadn't been getting enough rest. The constant ripping and running in the streets was catching up to him.

Raekwon got out the bed and walked to the bathroom to take a piss. He pulled his family jewel out of his boxers and leaned over the toilet with his left hand on the wall to hold him up. He closed his eyes and tried to let nature take its course, but to his surprise, there was a delay. Raekwon's eyes quickly widened.

Suddenly, piss shot out uncontrollably, splashing on the shower door and drizzling on the bathroom floor. He felt a slight numbness and a burning sensation all at the same time. Raekwon was embarrassed of himself.

He walked out of the bathroom and sat down on the bed. Lost in his thoughts, he made countless facial expression that revealed the fuming rage he was feeling inside. *Punk-ass bitch,* he thought to himself when he figured out who did it.

After taking a long shower, he threw on his clothes, grabbed his car keys, and headed for the back door. It seemed like everything he did was in fast forward. He hopped in the car and headed for the clinic.

As Raekwon drove, his frustration was focused on Tracy. She was the one he took to the hotel a couple of nights ago. He was real cool with her and had never fucked her until that night when they got real drunk. She surprised him when she seduced him into taking a shower with her, only after catching her man with another woman.

Tracy damn near drank a fifth of Hennessy all to herself like it was water, and that night, he found out she was extremely aggressive. After he took a shower with her, she stepped out and grabbed him by the hand, leading him to the bedroom of the hotel.

Her smooth chocolate complexion, thick thighs, and firm titties were irresistible. She was a sex goddess in so many ways. Her light brown eyes had him hypnotized. He couldn't turn that pussy down if he wanted to.

With both of their bodies dripping wet, she pushed him backwards onto the bed and began pleasuring him as if his dick was the last dick she was ever going to have the opportunity to suck again. It was a trip how females would get mad at their men and give the pussy away to the next dude who they thought had a little money. That night, he found out there was a freak behind that innocent smile. It was true that the finest females were the freakiest.

As he neared the clinic, he picked up his cell phone and

dialed Tracy's number.

"Hello."

"What the fuck you doin'?" Raekwon bitterly asked when she answered.

"Why you askin' me like that?"

"'Cause a nigga mad than a muthafucka, that's why," he recklessly responded.

"What's wrong?" Her curiosity level was high.

"Bitch, you burned me," he blurted through gritted teeth.

There was silence.

Raekwon broke the stillness with rudeness. "What the fuck you gettin' quiet for now?"

Tracy's voice was submissive. "I ain't. What you mean? And why you callin' me out of my name?"

"What the fuck you mean, what I mean? Yo' punk ass gave a nigga the claps or somethin', hoe. You ain't realize yo' pussy was on fire?" His rhetorical rudeness was very keen.

She began to sob. "I'm sorry. I didn't know."

He had no compassion for her feelings. "Bitch, fuck you. If I ever see yo' punk ass in the lanes, I'm gonna beat yo' ass."

He hung up the phone.

After his embarrassing visit to the clinic, he went straight to the house, where he sat for a couple of days to clear his system and collect his thoughts. He didn't have the attitude or the energy to be in traffic.

Raekwon had been a little wary of the law lately. He was keeping a close eye on their actions, and at the same time, hoping they weren't doing the same with him. Everything was happening so fast, and he couldn't keep letting his actions insinuate that he couldn't be touched. His conscience was eating at him with the truth, but his mind was playing tricks on him.

Tone had been out in the lanes heavy, getting his money. His Mexican connection was showing him all the love that he could ask for. He told Raekwon that he was the only black dude that they would do business with. Every time he copped, Raekwon got blessed. He needed to control his splurging, but he wasn't going to let the dudes in the hood that were getting money outshine him. It was an ego thing.

There was a rapper named Black Polo that was having a record release party. The whole day had been festive, and they were rolling pretty deep. Raekwon, Dre, Donnie, Bodine, Cray, Elgin, Meko, Buddy, Cal, Carlos, Kel, Tip, and Black Eddy were all in Raekwon's basement trying to figure out who was going to ride with who. They all hopped in four different cars, and trailed each other to the event. As they hit Colfax, Raekwon got on his cell phone and called Tone.

"Hello," Tone answered.

In the background, all Raekwon could hear was what sounded like hundreds of people's voices trying to talk over the loud music playing.

"Damn, that shit must be crackin', huh?" Raekwon asked.

"Hell yeah. Where y'all niggas at?" Tone was talking so loud that Raekwon had to hold the phone away from his ear.

"We way down the Fax, but we gonna be there in a minute, though."

They hung up.

"Let me hit that blunt, nigga," Raekwon said, while looking into his rearview mirror to the back seat where Elgin was babysitting the weed in silence.

After Elgin passed him the weed, he hit it a couple of times

178

and then glanced over at Bodine, who was in the passenger seat dozing off. Raekwon tapped him on the shoulder to pass him the weed.

"Nigga, wake yo' drunk ass up."

Bodine quickly sat up. "I ain't sleep, nigga."

"Yeah, whatever. Here, grab this weed." After he passed him the weed, Raekwon stared at the outside surroundings.

Colfax was a long demoralized strip. It seemed like it never ended, and that was for two reasons. Everybody drove below the speed limit to avoid attracting attention from the abundance of police that patrolled the boulevard. There was also the fact that they couldn't help but notice all the funny-looking people that were always into all kinds of suspicious activities. Anything they could think of under the sun happened on Colfax.

There were dopefiends and streetwalkers trying to flag them down, which wasn't unusual. Police were parked in dark alleys and sitting in parking lots with theirs lights off, waiting for undercover operations to take place. The scene was bizarre. Raekwon rarely liked to drive down Colfax, but he was legit. Besides, the back streets took longer due to all of the stop signs.

As they approached the theater where the show was being held, the traffic was jammed. Dudes were hanging out of big bodies and SUV's trying to get a glimpse of all of the females that were standing out in the front waiting to get inside.

Raekwon searched for somewhere to park. The parking lots were full, so they were forced to park in the lot of a nearby Taco Bell.

They got out of the car and crossed the street. The lobby of the place was crammed with people waiting in line to give their ticket to the lady at the window. There was also quite a few police standing in the lobby. Raekwon noticed Vamp dressed in street clothes and walked up to him.

"What the fuck you doin' at a rap concert in regular clothes? You must think a muthafucka ain't gonna know you the police or somethin', huh?" Raekwon laughed.

Vamp was working an undercover operation.

"I guess now I gotta leave since so many of you know who the fuck I am. I can't seem to get away from you guys," Vamp responded with irritation.

Raekwon walked off without responding. It wasn't cool to be standing there conversing with the police. When he walked back over to where his homies were standing, he noticed some commotion nearby.

Meko looked agitated. He shook his head and sighed. "See them bitches right there?" he asked while pointing. "The ones that just left the front of the line said these muthafuckas told them that they ain't lettin' nobody else in 'cause it's too packed."

All of a sudden, the police began trying to clear out the lobby. Everybody refused to leave, saying they had paid their money and wasn't going anywhere. The lobby was loud with everyone yelling, "Fuck the police!"

Raekwon noticed a couple of police passing messages to each other while spreading out in different corners of the lobby. He had no idea what was going on, but it looked suspicious. A couple of dudes got subdued and put in handcuffs for running off at the mouth a little too much.

"Aw shit!" a short, stocky nigga yelled, while holding his right hand over his face and running towards the lobby door.

When everybody noticed the police had started pulling out pepper spray, they all rushed towards the exit like a herd of cattle.

Because of all of the drama that was going down in the lobby, the police made the owner of the theater shut the show down. Colfax was blocked off with police that were trying to run everybody off. The fast-food restaurants had several tow trucks dragging people's cars off for occupying private parking.

Raekwon quickly glanced over at the Taco Bell. "Damn! Them muthafuckas is hookin' my shit up to they truck," he said to nobody in particular, while running across the street. "Hey! Hold up! That's my shit!" he yelled as he approached the oily-looking white man.

"I'm just following orders, sir. I'll unhook you for twenty dollars, 'cause if your car woulda been lifted up already, I woulda had to charge you forty," the white guy in his late thirties told him with a serious look.

After rescuing his car, Raekwon saw Bodine and Elgin running towards the parking lot. Police had flooded the entire area with billy clubs in their hands because things had gotten a little out of hand with the bottles flying at patrol cars. Mostly everybody had already evacuated the scene, and he wasn't going to be caught up in the middle of all the drama.

They pulled off into traffic following all of the other cars that were leaving the event. It was evident they weren't following each other by coincidence.

While Bodine reached in the ashtray for the half of blunt, he told Raekwon, "I saw Tone and Mondo coming out of the theater. They said the after party is at the Belgian Square."

"Oh yeah? That's where all these muthafuckas is goin' then.

Shit, I'ma just follow these bitches in front of us." Raekwon was glad the night wasn't over because it was too early for that.

When they pulled into the parking lot of the Belgian, there was a lot of people standing outside of their cars, talking and drinking. The scene seemed more relaxed. It was on the other side of town, and there were no police in sight.

Raekwon was a little tipsy and high, but the bar was the first thing on his mind. When he stepped inside the building, he felt the presence of respect. He wasn't worried about enemies because he didn't have many. Although a few of his associates had a couple of enemies lingering around, he didn't really sweat it. Everybody was in their own crowded conversations, eyes glowing and dressed like ghetto celebrities. The scene had a formal presence to it with a touch of street mannerism.

The Belgian was a very classy place. There were crystal chandeliers hanging from the ceiling just above the several tables that sat in parallel rows that were equally proportioned and covered with wedding white tablecloths with designer lace trimming. There was an uncovered doorway about twelve-feet wide that led to the hardwood dance floor area, and nearby the bar was crowded.

The voices struggled to talk over the fine selection of music being played by the DJ. There was a flight of stairs that curved up to a balcony area where most people were ducking the security in order to smoke their weed.

Most of the dudes had on their best jewelry and outfits, with freshly groomed faces. Raekwon was right in where he fitted, except his peach fuzz wasn't mature enough to be trimmed up yet. However, keeping up with his peers in the fashion department wasn't hard at all because he had been collecting easy money.

Spotting Black Eddy and JC at the bar buying drinks, Raekwon walked over to them.

"What's up, niggas?" His greeting was with confidence, like he had the world in his palm.

There were a couple of classy little chicks standing close enough to smell the scent of a dude's body wash. By observing their demeanor, he could almost convict them of being sack chasers, which about eighty percent of them were, if not more.

"Damn, y'all smell like strawberry daiquiris," Black Eddy said to the ladies, while leaning back on the bar with his drink in his hand. His head was tilted into his chest, almost as if he was undressing the both of them with his eyes. "How can I get the taste of yo' mouth in my mouth?"

His humor seemed too absurd to the two women, as they gave him a dry look without responding and walked off. Black Eddy was drunk, and when he got drunk in this type of environment, it was like having to look after a child in a candy store. He had enemies from his involvement with gangs, and Raekwon was pretty sure his enemies were somewhere close.

Raekwon reached in his pocket, pulling out a wad of money. He flicked two, one hundred dollar bills on the bar's surface.

"Let me get a tab, fella," he said arrogantly to the bartender. He added a loose twenty dollar bill as a tip. "Put that in ya' lil' pocket and let me get two double shots of Henny for now." He had a way of gaining respect when he dealt with people. His presence alone made it difficult for a person to not take a liking to him in some kind of way.

He moved through the crowd, conversing with dudes that he knew and flirting with girls that he wanted to get to know better.

In the process of making his rounds, he came up on a couple of phone numbers. He heard a familiar voice call his name though the crowd of sweating and aspiring sex symbols. The lights were dim, but it didn't really make it hard for him to see across the room.

Tone waved for him to come over to where he and Mondo were chilling alongside where the DJ was staged at.

"Over here, nigga!" Tone yelled loud enough for Raekwon to hear him over the music and loud conversations.

Raekwon walked up and said, "Damn, I ain't even know y'all niggas was in here all this time."

"Yeah, we been in here for about a hour or somethin' hollerin' at these gold-diggin' hoes with the shoes to match they hats," Tone replied, then took a sip out of the pint of Hennessy that he was holding. "I seen you over there at the bar earlier, buyin' that high-priced shit. You shoulda brought ya own shit like I did."

"We drank all that shit up on the way here." Raekwon rubbed his hands together with a smirk on his face. "Y'all niggas ain't hook up no hoes for the night?"

"Hell yeah," Tone said. "I'm gonna get some head from Lashaun, the stinky stripper. That bitch probably sittin' in front of my house waitin' for me right now. I lied and told that stupid-ass bitch that I was on my way about an hour ago." He let out a light laugh while shaking his head.

Meko walked up and sighed. "Kwon, you need to help me get that nigga Black Ed. He got all the hoes in the place mad. That nigga been grabbin' bitches by the ass and gettin' mad when they cuss his ass out. That nigga is toooo drunk." He exaggerated his last couple of words in order to make Raekwon understand the severity of what he was telling him.

Raekwon asked, "Where's that nigga at?"

"He up there on that balcony laid out in the bathroom. The homies is wit' him, though," Meko said, while pointing upstairs.

"Man, y'all need to take that nigga home or somethin'. He gonna get some shit started," Tone said. "Watch and see what I tell you." His expression was serious.

Meko looked at Tone and said, "Get some shit started? He done already been up there arguing wit' some nigga about the nigga's baby momma. He knows he wrong, but he arguing wit' muthafuckas like he right, and it turned into some gangbangin' shit after that."

Raekwon didn't have a good feeling about what he heard from Meko. He damn near sobered up after that. It was always something Black Eddy was caught in between. Raekwon wouldn't dare leave his homey hanging. Being that Black Eddy was a gang banger, it compromised his association with people that he didn't get along with. He made enemies like the earth produced water.

When Meko and Raekwon got upstairs, there was some commotion. They made their way through the crowded area, only to find Cal and Dre holding Black Eddy back from some dude that Polo and a few others were trying to calm down.

Polo walked up to Raekwon with steam leaking from the corners of his eyes. "Y'all need to get that nigga, man. He done got some bullshit started. This is my shit, and if somethin' happens, I'ma be responsible and get fined for it. I don't know what's wrong wit' that nigga, but he got a whole lot of people mad. My bitch said the nigga grabbed her ass, but I didn't trip because of the respect I got for you and Tone. That's y'all people."

Everybody in the place began to take notice of what was going on. Security came upstairs and told them that the owner of the building wanted everybody out. There was no fuss about it. Black folks couldn't have anything without disrespecting each other. That's what the older cats always said when Raekwon was growing up, and it was true.

Everybody was exiting the Belgian, and it started to get loud as the parking lot filled up. Raekwon watched as the dudes that Black Eddy got into it with quickly began walking towards their cars. He lost sight of them as more and more people began coming outside, blocking his view.

"Bitch, fuck you and yo' punk-ass nigga!" a thick, dark-skinned broad yelled, while taking off one of her shoes. She got hit in the mouth before she had a chance to take off the other shoe.

All Raekwon could hear was ooh's and aah's, while titties fell out of bras and skirts flew up. One nigga yelled, "Look, that bitch ain't got no panties on." Somebody was getting their ass whooped, but Raekwon knew it wasn't the chick that took off her shoe first just by the sounds of it. He couldn't see what was going on after the large crowd shifted into his narrow view.

"Somebody tell this bitch to let my hair go. Bitch, let my hair go!" the thick, dark-skinned girl yelled.

After security broke up the fight, everybody walked away laughing and describing how everything went down. Raekwon saw JC and a couple of dudes from their hood trying to wrestle a pistol out of Black Eddy's hand. People that were in the vicinity started walking in the opposite direction when they noticed.

"Fuck that shit! I'ma smoke that nigga! Where cuz go?" Black Eddy yelled in reference to the dude that he got into it with inside the Belgian. He was trying to wrestle his way out of JC's arms that were wrapped around him from behind.

There was a loud uproar throughout the parking lot. Raekwon noticed Tone and Mondo standing over by Tone's Benz. Mondo looked around suspiciously. Raekwon looked in the direction that Mondo was staring as he walked towards his car, hoping that Elgin and Bodine would hurry up. He was a little nervous because it was hard to read what was actually going to transpire.

A dark blue Suburban pulled into the parking lot, and the window of the passenger side began to roll down.

Boom! Mondo let off a shot into the sky that caused seconds of silence. Then shots began ringing off everywhere after that.

Raekwon ran towards the first car he saw and crouched down as low as he could. His eyes immediately converted his peripheral vision into tunnel vision that could see nothing but a getaway. The door on the car was open, so he lay on the ground and crawled under it. He felt like he was part of the army infantry unit, without a gun.

"Lay yo' ass down!" he yelled with aggression.

Janice, Big Vic's cousin, was peeking over the dashboard of her car, trying to see what was going on. She quickly lay across the front seat after screaming out of fear. She didn't notice Raekwon sneak up on her car. She was four months pregnant and had no business being there anyway.

All he could hear was what sounded like six or seven different guns firing. The screams that echoed crawled up his spine like ants as car doors slammed and tires peeled off. Raekwon was drunk and didn't know whether he was coming or going. It was every man for himself.

After the gunshots ceased, most of the cars that were in the parking lot sped off. The moment was intense. He slowly pushed his body up and on to one knee. He couldn't see beyond the open car door that was in front of him.

Raekwon tapped Janice on the leg. "Is you alright, girl?"

"Is everybody gone yet?" she asked, not bothering to budge.

"Shit, I guess so," he slurred dryly.

"Who the fuck is that over there laid out in the parking lot?" somebody shouted out while walking to their car with a couple of other people.

Janice sat up and looked out of her front windshield. "Oh no! Is that Magic?" she screamed at the top of her lungs, with her hand trembling across her mouth. She eased out of the car, biting on her fingernails.

Raekwon's eyes widened as he stood up. "Where at?"

Janice panicked as she pointed and started screaming. "Over there! Over there! That is Magic! That's him!" Her screams broke down into uncontrollable cries as they neared where Magic lay shaking on the ground.

Magic was the father of Janice's unborn child. Raekwon had heard a lot about him, but never got the chance to actually meet him in person. He had been trying to hook up with him through Big Vic to do some music, but one of them was always busy.

Raekwon walked his drunken ass over to where Magic laid. His eyes were rolling into the back of his head. He didn't want to accept the fact that he was dying from a gunshot wound. Raekwon grabbed him by one of his hands.

"Come on, homie. Get up. Let's go," he said, while trying to lift him up off of the ground.

Magic didn't respond. Raekwon didn't give up until he noticed a river of blood rushing from the back of his head. He was instantly traumatized as a tear rolled down his cheek. He stood over Magic's dying body, frozen and in silence. Most of Raekwon's emotions came from being drunk.

"Is he dead? Is he dead?" Janice yelled.

Raekwon didn't respond. He just stood there dazed.

"Move out the way!" a white police woman yelled as she ran towards Magic's body.

Janice pulled Raekwon's shirt from behind. "Come on," she cried. "There's nothing we can do but let them try to help him." She stared at the other police officers with envy. "What the fuck took y'all so fuckin' long? If he was a cracker, y'all woulda been here a long time ago."

Keeping his composure, one of the officers said, "Please stand back, lady."

A couple of Janice's friends walked up to help comfort her. Raekwon asked her was she going to be alright before walking with a slow pace back to his car. As he approached the car, he noticed Bodine sitting in the passenger seat.

Raekwon pulled the driver door open. "How long you been sittin' in here?"

"Shit, man, I been in this muthafucka sleep for I don't know how long. I was so drunk that I just left up out of that muthafucka a little bit after we first got here. Them gunshots woke me up."

"Where that nigga Elgin at?" Raekwon asked.

"When we first got here, that nigga said he was gonna hop in the car wit' Cray and them on the way back."

On the ride home, Raekwon told Bodine everything that happened inside and outside of the Belgian. It was a trip to reflect back on the chain of events that took place. He sped home, running through red lights as if the law didn't exist. He was disturbed because he hated to see innocent dudes die over stupid stuff that could've been avoided.

Raekwon dropped Bodine off and went home. He couldn't seem to get comfortable enough to go to sleep. So, he laid face up, watching the ceiling, lost in thought until he inferred himself to sleep. Raekwon had no dreams, just nightmares.

THE DYNASTY
&
DISASTER

CHAPTER 13

Raekwon woke up late in the day to the sound of the phone ringing. He didn't want to answer it, but the perpetual rings made him assume the call may be important.

"Hello," he answered in a dry voice.

"Boy, what you doin' sleep?" Roxanne's powerful voice echoed through the receiver.

"Shit, I'm getting up now," he said recklessly.

"Who you think you talking to? Boy, don't think you can cuss around me just 'cause I don't live there no mo'. I know you growin' up, but I'm still yo' momma, negro," she said in a agitated manner.

His instincts kicked in. "My fault, Mom."

There were a few seconds of silence.

"Boy, what's wrong wit' you? You sure been actin' funny lately. You don't even call yo' po' momma no mo'."

Raekwon's voice rose. "I do call you. I—"

She cut him off. "Naw, ya don't either. Don't even sit up there and tell that lie. Boy, you been actin' kinda funny. You need to bring yo' butt to church 'cause the devil is really workin' on you."

"What you mean I been actin' funny? I ain't been actin' funny, and I planned on comin' to church wit' you Sunday."

She smacked her lips. "Yeah right. You said that about two Sundays ago, and I ain't heard from you since. I don't know what I'll do if God didn't give me the strength to pray for y'all. Y'all just done forgot about y'all's po' momma. Don't do nuttin' to try to help me out. Y'all don't care about nobody but y'all self. You and ya brother both."

Raekwon didn't respond because he didn't want to argue with her. He felt differently than what she was saying, but his opinion never mattered with her.

Once again, there was silence.

"I'll talk to you later since you over there trippin'," she finally said and then hung up in his face.

Ten minutes later, the phone rang again, but he didn't answer it. Next, his pager went off. When he looked at the display, it was Tone's number followed with the code 9-1-1. Raekwon picked up the phone. He was eager to find out what the emergency was about.

"Hello."

"What's up?" Raekwon said with curiosity in his voice.

"Where you at?" Tone asked.

"Shit, I'm at the crib layin' down."

"I just called over there," Tone replied, trying to control the agitation in his voice.

"Yeah, I know. I thought it was somebody else. What's happenin'?"

"You know that muthafuckas been runnin' around sayin' we

had somethin' to do wit' that shit that happened to Magic," he said seriously.

"Huh? How they come up wit' some shit like that? We was duckin' under cars and shit just like everybody else."

"I think it was 'cause of all the muthafuckas that was mad at Black Ed. They said he did it. You know how muthafuckas be hatin' on niggas."

"That nigga didn't even shoot the pistol he was holdin' 'cause JC took it from him," Raekwon said in a defensive manner.

Tone sighed. "I know. We just gotta be strapped and be careful until we get this shit straightened out. I'ma hit you back later, though, 'cause my other line is beepin'."

The phone rang again not even thirty minutes after Raekwon hung up with Tone.

"Damn, now who the fuck is this?" he asked himself out loud, while picking up the phone. "Who 'dis?"

"Dis Pookie, nigga." His voice didn't seem to have any life to it.

Pookie was a real cool dude that Raekwon grew up around. He was a couple of years older than Pookie. Raekwon was caught up in that gangbanging shit, running with Bloods. He got along with a lot of Crips through hustling with them. Pookie's mom was a dopefiend, and he was a sherm head. He was a down-ass nigga in more ways than one. He used to give Raekwon fat-ass double-ups when he couldn't get any anywhere else.

"What's wrong wit' you nigga?" Raekwon asked.

"You heard what happened to my relative Lil' Fred?"

Raekwon rolled out the bed and sat on the edge of it. "Naw.

What happened?" he asked, clutching the phone.

Pookie sighed. "I guess the lil' nigga got fed up or somethin'. You know that lil' white broad that he had a baby by?"

"Yeah."

"He took the bitch, parked on the side of the highway, killed her, and pushed her body out the car. I guess he started thinkin' about goin' back to jail 'cause he drove a lil' farther down the highway, pulled over, and killed himself in the car."

"Damn, that shit is crazy, homie." Raekwon sighed and shook his head in shame.

"I know, man," Pookie continued. "When they found 'em the next morning, they daughter was in the back seat strapped to her carseat, cryin'. She was in the muthafuckin' car all night. That lil' girl gonna be traumatized from that shit," he stressed with intense emotion.

"I know you sick about that shit. I'ma be prayin' for y'all family, my nigga."

"Yeah, we'll get through it. Shit, I'm finna go over here to his momma's house, so I'ma get wit' you, though."

"Fa' sho," Raekwon said before they hung up.

Raekwon was in juvenile hall with Lil' Fred. He used to be a wild, stubborn dude. He was always getting into fights with others over the phone. He always talked about how he wasn't ever going back to jail for nothing. He said they would never take him back to their alive. Raekwon was able to see just what he meant.

Dehydrated, Raekwon got up and went upstairs to get some orange juice. His step-dad, Ben, was sitting at the kitchen table bagging up some dope into eightballs. He had started being absent from the house more.

"I see you done finally got up," Ben said.

"Yeah, I was tired." Raekwon leaned on the counter by the microwave, drinking his orange juice.

"You ain't seen yo' brother, have you?" Ben looked at him with anticipation.

"I ain't seen that nigga since yesterday. Why?" he asked.

"He was supposed to have done somethin' for me, but I can't get in touch wit' him. See, the dude I usually get my stuff from been out of town. He 'posed to be bringin' me one of them birds back 'cause I already gave him the money. I need a couple of ounces to hold me off for a couple of days. You know somebody I can get 'em from?

Raekwon looked at him strangely because he had never dealt with him before when it came to business. "Uh, I can hit Tone for you real quick."

"Oh yeah? I ain't know he had it goin' on like that or I woulda been hollered at him."

After that day, Ben and Tone dealt with each other on a regular basis. Raekwon was doing his own thing and taking in the slow dope money just to be cautious. After Ben learned of all the drama that was going on, he gave Raekwon an extra pistol and told him to page him if anything happened. Raekwon already knew there was an AK and a Mac 11 that he kept upstairs in the backroom closet.

Raekwon got up early in the morning to go to The Market and grab some blunts. He could tell it was a nice day outside by the way the sun was beaming through his window. He was supposed to kick it with Portia later on and go out to eat with her.

He finally had hooked up with her and made her his woman a few months back. They had been through a couple of arguments and fights, but that was all written in the fine print of having a relationship.

Raekwon stepped outside. As he was locking the door, Portia pulled up across the street. She had her windows down and her factory car stereo up.

Portia turned down the volume on her stereo. "Where you 'bout to go?"

"To the store real quick," he responded nonchalantly.

"What's wrong with yo' car?" Her face was screwed up with confusion.

"Nothing." Raekwon glanced at his car as he made his way down the driveway. "Why you say that?" he asked.

"Yes, it is. Yo' tires over on this side is flat."

He looked at her in disbelief. "Flat?" Raekwon walked around to the side of the car and saw it for himself. "What the fuck?"

Portia asked the wrong question at the wrong time. "Who did that?" She made a puzzled face while still in the car.

Raekwon snapped. "What the fuck you mean who did it? I don't know. If I knew, I woulda did somethin' about it already. Yo' ass probably did it for all I know."

"Nigga, what you mean I probably did it? One of them stupid lil' bitches you been fuckin' wit' behind my back probably did it."

"What bitches? I don't know what the fuck you talking 'bout. Girl, you trippin' now. Anybody coulda did that shit." He realized he couldn't just blame her like that, or could he?

Raekwon walked up to the tires and noticed the slits in

them. Every possible reason why someone would do that ran across his mind. Maybe it was a death threat or maybe it was some chick. *Niggas don't usually do shit like this,* he reasoned. He came to the conclusion that it had to be the work of a jealous bitch, but who, he didn't know. He had fucked so many of them without commitments that he would never know without a confession or eyewitness.

Portia ended up taking him to purchase some tires. They argued the whole way there and drove the whole way back in silence. When they got back to the house, he put his new tires on.

Right before he hopped inside his car to look for his license in the glove box, Portia asked with a mean face and a dry voice, "I thought we was still gonna chill today?"

Raekwon looked at her like she was stupid. "I ain't takin' yo' stupid-ass no muthafuckin' where."

"Fuck it! I'll just go by myself then. And I ain't stupid either!" she yelled out the window and drove off.

Raekwon was glad she was gone. He ran into the house to wash his hands and then went back out to the car to finish looking for his license. He was still mad, but he wasn't going to let it get in the way of his focus.

Raekwon noticed the sound of a car engine humming down the block. Out of instinct, he sat up and looked in his rearview mirror. He saw a sky blue Lumina approaching slowly. He hadn't seen the car before, so he became suspicious of the way it was creeping up the block. He always clocked the cars that frequented his block, and this wasn't one of them.

The car slowed down by the speed bumps a house away. Raekwon stood up out of his car and closed the door. A dark-skinned dude pulled mean-mugging him. The dude glanced in Raekwon's car as Raekwon made his way around to the other side.

Raekwon had never seen the dude before, and his body sensed trouble as he leaned on the passenger side of his car facing the street. Raekwon gave him a distraught look as the dude sat in his car looking his way.

"Hey, homie, you know where Raekwon live at?"

Raekwon's insides froze up on him. His question sent chills of anxiety through his body. That sounded like the first time Raekwon had ever heard his name called, and it also felt like it would be the last.

He gave him a "what's up" nod and asked, "Why? Who wanna know?" Raekwon began walking up the sidewalk to his front door while closely observing the dude's every movement.

Raekwon looked down the block both directions as quickly as he could and then turned his focus back on the dude as he reached the front door. He stood halfway in the house with the screen door open.

He looked at him with suspicion and asked, "You're Raekwon, ain't you?"

"Why you wanna know?" By now, Raekwon's adrenaline was rushing with anxiety.

"Don't worry about that. Just come here real quick and let me holler at you." Through the evil grit on his face, Raekwon could assume his intentions were detrimental.

Raekwon looked up and down the block again. "If you got somethin' to say, you can say it from right there."

"Why you keep lookin' up and down the block?" When the dude looked out of his windshield, he noticed Dre standing in the middle of his yard a few houses down. He looked the other way and saw Kel standing on one of the neighbor's wooden fences. After the dude saw them posted, he began to ease off of his brakes. "Oh, y'all niggas is deep, huh?" He nodded his head. "So y'all the muthafuckas who killed my lil' cousin Magic!" he yelled as he slowed up at the corner.

Raekwon ran out into the street. "We ain't kill no muthafuckin' body, nigga! I ain't even have no pistol that night!" he yelled down the block.

The dude pulled his car sideways at the corner and yelled back, "You passed the strap to yo' homeboy Black Eddy and he did it."

Raekwon snapped. "I ain't pass that nigga shit, and he wasn't shootin' anyway. That was some other niggas who did that shit."

"Who did it then?" he asked from a distance.

"I don't know."

When the car looked as if it was going to make a U-turn, Raekwon ran in the house and to the back room. He opened the closet door and quickly grabbed the AK that was in a military case. His insides exploded with anger as tears overflowed his eyes.

"I'm tired of this shit!" he yelled, while unzipping the bag to reveal the assault rifle. He grabbed one of the many banana clips that filled the pockets surrounding the case.

His hands shook nervously as he clutched the AK. He loaded the clip, cocked the rifle, and proceeded back towards the front door. Raekwon wiped the tears from his eyes with his shirt as he stood in front of the doorway holding the AK. His heart pounded what felt like a ton of fury. When he looked around, the dude was nowhere in sight. Raekwon swore to himself that he was going to light up the whole block if he was still there. He didn't care anymore. Patience didn't live inside him at that point, and nothing mattered at all.

Kel and Dre walked up to the screen door as Raekwon was calming himself down. His sense of reality had returned from being warped into the zone of a madman.

Dre swung the door open and walked in. He glanced at the rifle leaning up against the wall and then at Raekwon. "Nigga, what the fuck is goin' on?" he asked.

Raekwon shook his head unconvincingly. "Nothin'. I'm cool."

Kel put his cigarette out on the porch with his foot while holding the screen door open. He walked in the house and asked, "Who was that nigga yellin' up the block in the sky blue car?"

Raekwon's bitterness had his mind in its own district. He stared at the floor, sat on the arm of the couch, and gritted his teeth. He yanked his head and blurted, "I'm tired of these niggas!"

Raekwon told Kel and Dre everything that had happened. Neither of them had ever seen the dude before either. They wondered who had sent him in the right direction to find where Raekwon lived. It had to be a close source, but who it was, he had no idea.

They strapped up and combed the streets to find the dude, but to no avail. So, they decided to go to the liquor store and slide by Kel's house. They were trying to ease the tension that was present among them.

After chilling with Dre and Kel for a while and getting a

little drunk, Raekwon called Tone and told him that he needed to holler at him. Tone told Raekwon that he would meet him at his house in a couple of hours. Before going home, Raekwon made a couple of stops to collect some money that was owed to him.

Raekwon paced back and forth in the kitchen impatiently until he heard a car pulling up in front of the house. He peeked out of the living room window and saw Tone walking up to the house with Mondo. Raekwon unlocked the door and opened it before they had a chance to knock.

"What's up, nigga?" Tone asked as he walked to the kitchen with Mondo trailing behind him.

Raekwon locked the door and followed closely behind. He walked into the kitchen and released a forceful sigh. "Man…" There was suspense behind the presence of his gesture.

"Why you say that?" Tone asked.

Raekwon paused and sat down at the kitchen table. He explained to him what had happened in front of the house earlier in the day. His mood had no excitement to it.

"I knew some shit like that was gonna happen sooner or later. Let one of them niggas roll up on me like that and I'ma kill one of them muthafuckas. Nigga, I told you to keep yo' heat wit' you 'cause these niggas running around here spreadin' that fake-ass rumor. That nigga coulda killed you, and then what?"

Raekwon put his head down and began shaking it. "I know, man." He didn't have anything to say back because he knew Mono was speaking the truth.

Mondo asked, "You got a pistol, don't you?"

"Yeah, I got a pistol," Raekwon stressed.

"'Cause you can't take that AK everywhere you go,"

Mondo replied, acting as if he was concerned.

Tone asked. "Where Ben at?"

"I don't even know. I ain't seen him all day. You know that nigga don't never be here anyway," Raekwon replied.

"Damn, that nigga was supposed to meet me here so he could grab these nine ounces." Tone laid his pistol and keys on the counter, then pulled a large Ziploc bag full of cocaine from the waistline of his pants. "Fuck it. I'll just cook this shit up and have you hold it for him."

"Hook up four of 'em for me, too." Raekwon pulled his money out of his pocket and began counting it.

After looking inside of every cabinet in the kitchen, Tone asked, "Where Ben put all the cookin' jars?"

Raekwon gave a confused look. "Shit, I don't even know. He probably got them muthafuckas wit' him knowin' his ass."

"Damn, I got one at the crib, but I don't feel like drivin' no more wit' all this shit on me." Tone sighed. I'ma chill out after I get rid of all this shit. I just escaped a little traffic warrant last night. If I wouldn't had used my brother's name, I woulda been hit for like a year. I got warrants, and this game got a nigga paranoid 'cause it's hot right now."

"You ain't said nothing, nigga," Raekwon started. "I been feeling the same way for some reason."

"Shit, I been feelin' like a muthafucka's been following me around and some mo' shit," Tone said. "It's like a nigga be knowin' when some shit ain't right, but don't listen to his first instincts for some reason. I'ma listen to my shit this time."

"Me, too," Raekwon agreed.

"Fuck what y'all talking about!" Mondo exclaimed. "I gotta get this money, man."

Tone responded, "Nigga, you don't ever listen. Always bein' hardheaded. That's the reason why yo' ass got to go to court now."

They sat around talking for about an hour and a half waiting for Ben to show up, but he never did.

"Fuck it. I'ma just hook up wit' him tomorrow or something. Matter of fact, just meet me at the house in about two hours and I should be done. You can grab this shit for Ben, too," Tone told Raekwon, then grabbed his pistol and keys off of the counter.

After Tone and Mondo left, Raekwon went downstairs to think. He wanted to be alone. He couldn't seem to see past the misery he was living through. It made him think of suicide in a not so serious way. Two hours later, tired and tipsy, he fell asleep against his own will.

The next morning, Raekwon woke up with a knot in his stomach. His anxieties mixed with the smell of alcohol on his breath had taken a toll on him. The contractions in his bowels that overpowered the choices he had been granted as a human being had him in submission.

He took deep breaths and slow steps while holding his stomach the whole way to the bathroom. He felt miserable and didn't have enough room in his throbbing head to think straight. Raekwon spent nearly an hour on the toilet, in which the sweating walls seemed to have stole every breath of fresh air that snuck its way through the crack of the basement bathroom window.

After relieving himself, he remembered he was supposed to go grab the dope from Tone last night. He hurried to the phone.

Raekwon called Tone's cell phone three times back to back,

but it went straight to voicemail after the first ring every time. Raekwon assumed he could be on his other line, so he decided to page him to his cell phone.

Raekwon didn't bother taking a shower or even brushing his teeth. He had to catch up with Tone before he got into traffic and forgot about the fact that Raekwon had no dope to supply the hungry hustlers of the streets with. He grabbed his car keys, snatched his cell phone up off of the dresser, and made his way to the back door.

As he drove through the city, the wind gained a forceful speed and began to whistle through the front grill of his car. The clouds overlapped the sun and gave the bright Wednesday the feeling of a boring Sunday. The clouds finally passed, but the wind remained angry.

Traffic was light. Raekwon enjoyed the drive. He had been spending a lot of time by himself lately, which was good because it sheltered him away from all of the distractions. It allowed him the opportunity to experience, but he would never find it if he couldn't find his way through The Maze.

After a twenty-minute drive, Raekwon pulled up in front of Tone's house. When he noticed his Benz wasn't parked in the driveway, Raekwon assumed he might have parked in the garage, which he did on rare occasions.

Raekwon cut the engine off and stepped out. He observed his surroundings while walking up to the front door. He knocked on the screen door for a couple of minutes but got no answer. *Maybe he got up early and left, or he probably didn't come home last night,* Raekwon thought to himself.

Raekwon started walking away from the door until he thought about how badly he needed those four ounces. His persistent hustling hand had turned him around.

"He might be sleep," Raekwon whispered to himself as he caught the idea.

He pulled the screen door open, and with one aggressive knock, the door slowly screeched open to a crack. He took a step back just because he became skeptical.

"What the fuck?"

He didn't immediately assume the worse until he noticed the door had been kicked open. Raekwon took two easy steps inside of Tone's house.

"Tone!" he yelled in a deep voice, while continuously looking in every direction.

Raekwon walked into the door that led him inside of Tone's garage. His Benz and his low-rider were not there. Raekwon stood and thought to himself, *Damn, did some muthafuckas come and rob this nigga or something?* Raekwon closed the door and slowly walked to the short flight of stairs that led to the second level of the house.

He cautiously walked up the stairs. He was a little paranoid. Something was terribly wrong with this picture and he didn't like one bit of it. His mind was racing, and his right hand was clutching the loaded pistol that was in his waistline.

Raekwon approached the living room area when he reached the top of the stairs. "Fuck!" he blurted out at the top of his lungs and put his left hand across his face. He leaned on the railing and massaged his temples.

The house was a mess. The tables and couches were flipped over, wall paintings were lying on the ground shattered, and Tone's big screen television was missing. There were several pairs of latex gloves scattered across the floor. He knew instantly that the police were involved.

Raekwon pulled himself together and walked up the second flight of stairs that led to Tone's bedroom. He didn't want to believe what he had just realized. He felt like the walls were closing in on him. His heart was racing. He stepped in Tone's room only to witness another excessive number of latex gloves laying everywhere. The bed was flipped, the sliding doors of the closet were leaning against the wall, and Tone's clothes and shoes was scattered across the room.

Raekwon hurried down the stairs and out of the house. All he could think about was the fact that they were most likely looking for him, too. As Raekwon exited the house, he couldn't help but scan the distance of the streets to see if any unmarked cars were still observing the house. He didn't notice anything suspicious. Maybe he was just being too paranoid, or maybe he was just naturally thinking the way a drug dealer was supposed to think.

The drive home was very intense for him. He had no idea of the scope of what was going on. Outraged, a single tear rolled down his cheek. He never pictured things happening this way.

He pulled up in front of his house and calmly stepped out of the car. He tried not to make it obvious that he had his eye out for any suspicious vehicles in the area. His heart was beating a thousand times a minute, but from the outside, one would've never been able to notice.

When Raekwon finally stepped inside of the house, he rushed down to the basement and into his bedroom. He got on his knees and reached under the bed, pulling from underneath it a pair of shoes that contained money inside of them. He put it in his pocket and rushed to the telephone.

"Hello," Bodine's sister answered.

"Hey, unlock the back door. I'm on my way over there." Raekwon hung up the phone before she could respond.

Raekwon felt like he was being overly suspicious in some way, which to him was a good way to be. Tone kept him away from the big runs and deals as much as he could. He couldn't seem to reason with himself enough to not think the worst case scenario.

Raekwon walked up the stairs and stepped outside. He grabbed a hold of his composure as he walked back to the car as if everything was normal. He convinced himself that if they really wanted him as bad as he was thinking, they would've come to get him when they got Tone.

When Raekwon hopped back inside of his car, he grabbed the pistol from under his seat and took the magazine full of bullets out of it. He released the bullet from the chamber, cleaned his fingerprints off of it, and slid it in the magazine. He put the magazine in his pants pockets, laid the pistol on his lap, and started up the car. Raekwon then pulled off slowly.

He hit a couple of corners and pulled up to a stop sign. He entered the four-way intersection, looking in all directions. His heart froze after he saw the unmarked car pulling off from two blocks down and coming towards his direction.

Out of instinct, he immediately pulled off. He was hoping the unmarked car would keep straight, but it turned and came after him. He watched in the rearview mirror. Raekwon sped up, trying to get around the car that was in front of him. He swerved to the left, and when the car in front of him began to make a left turn, he slammed on his brakes.

The officer was gaining on him. Raekwon made a quick

right with one hand on the steering wheel, while the other hand stuffed the pistol underneath the front seat. He sat up and watched the rearview mirror as the officer made the same right turn without stopping at the stop sign.

After making several abrupt turns, Raekwon pulled in front of Bodine's house and hopped out as quickly as he could, but it wasn't fast enough. He tried to walk up to the house as the officer hit the corner at high speed, stopped, and hopped out of his car.

"Excuse me, sir!" he yelled.

Raekwon played it cool and acted as if he never noticed him until now. Raekwon stopped and looked at him. "What's the problem, officer?"

The officer continued to walk towards him. "Do you have your license, vehicle registration, and insurance?"

Raekwon gave him an awkward look. What, you pullin' my shit over while it's parked or somethin'?"

"Well, sir, I was sent to identify the occupant of the vehicle. You were observed by our surveillance unit leaving the address we were instructed to issue a search warrant at. I was radioed with the description of your vehicle and have been following you for a couple of blocks."

Raekwon's adrenaline rushed. He reached in his back pocket, pulling out his wallet, and said, "That's my momma's car." He held his license out towards him and continued. "What y'all doin' a search warrant on that house for?"

The officer reached his hand out to get his license. "I can't discuss that information with you. Are you familiar with a person by the name of Benny Jamison aka Ben?"

"I can't discuss that information with you," Raekwon said

sarcastically after realizing they were in pursuit of his step-dad.

So you wanna be a smart ass, huh?" The officer then looked at his license and exclaimed, "Oh, the address on your identification matches that of the house you just left. So you live there, huh?"

"Yeah, I live at that house. That's why I just left there." Raekwon started to feel calm when it was evident that he was just being identified.

"Well, let me go run your name in the computer to make sure you're not wanted for anything, and then you can go if you don't have any warrants." He started to walk off, but Raekwon noticed he was glancing at his pocket out the corner of his eye. "What's that in your pocket?" he asked.

Raekwon patted his pocket. "Aw, that's just my cell phone." He pulled the cell out of his pocket to show him.

The officer looked at him suspiciously. "You don't have any narcotics on you, do you?"

Raekwon gave a convincing look in return. Naw, I don't deal drugs."

"Okay. Well, just let me pat you down real quick so I don't feel guilty about not following procedure."

Raekwon's body surrendered to his discouraging thoughts. He knew his suspicions would go sky high once he discovered the thousands of dollars and the magazine to the pistol that were in the pocket he kept at bay while talking to him from an angle. Raekwon turned with his back facing him and put his hands in the air.

The officer started patting at Raekwon's underarms and made his way down passed his waist line, then he clutched the contents of his right pocket.

"What's that right there?" he asked.

"Uhhhh, that's just..." Raekwon took off running and climbed a fence in an attempt to slow the officer down from pursuing him.

Since the officer had a rough time getting over the fence, Raekwon figured he could double back to the car and grab the pistol from under his seat so he could toss it.

Raekwon came sprinting around the corner and broke towards his car. He was nervous and out of breath. As Raekwon reached for the door handle on the driver's side, he slowed down.

"Hey, get back here!" the officer yelled, as he broke the corner, running through a yard.

Raekwon took off and slid through a broken fence on the side of Bodine's house. As he started to run around the house, he saw the officers coming in his direction. He turned around and ran back the other way, running back around to the front of the house. He stopped, reached in his pocket, and pulled out the magazine clip he had. Raekwon launched it as far as he could.

He then jogged over to the broken part of the fence where he heard a constant thrashing sound. The officer was trying to kick a larger hole in the wood so he could fit through the opening. When he saw Raekwon, he acted as if he was going to jump over the fence, but the top of the fence broke, which sent him falling to the ground on his back.

Raekwon hopped the fence that led to the yard next door. He was too tired to take off running, so he played the waiting game. He got up and ran next door to the gate's entrance. He tried to yank the door open, but it was locked.

"Open the fucking gate!" the Police ordered.

Raekwon was leaning forward with both hands on his knees, breathing hard. "I ain't did nothing," he said between breaths.

Raekwon stood up, looked over the fence, and noticed Bodine and his family frighteningly watching the confrontation from a window on the side of their house. Raekwon looked over his shoulder out of paranoia to make sure there weren't any cops closing in on him. He quickly turned back around towards the officers.

"Open the fucking gate!" This time, the officer made the demand while aiming the pistol between Raekwon's eyes.

"Damn! Alright! Alright! I ain't know it was that serious. You act like I killed somebody or somethin'," Raekwon said, with his hands in the air while walking towards the gate.

After Raekwon came from behind the gate, the officer told him to lay face down on the ground where he forced his knee in his back and put him in handcuffs. Moments later, several patrol cars and unmarked cars sped up the block and parked in front of Bodine's house.

Introducing himself to the other officers who arrived on the scene, the officer that had Raekwon in custody said, "Hello, I'm Agent Whitaker." Next, he looked at Raekwon and asked, "So, you're Raekwon, huh?"

Raekwon didn't respond.

"Where's the dope at, man?" Whitaker asked.

Raekwon looked up, sucked his teeth, and responded, "What dope? I don't know nuttin' 'bout no dope." Raekwon then looked at him like he was stupid.

Whitaker advised the officers to put him in the back of one of the patrol cars. Raekwon watched from the backseat as they searched his car and found the empty pistol under his front seat.

"Oh, what do we have here?" Whitaker asked rhetorically and sarcastically. "Take him down and process him for the possession of a concealed weapon." He walked up to the window of the patrol car and asked, "Where's the magazine to the gun? And where'd you get all the cash from?"

Raekwon cut his eyes at him without responding.

The ride to the police station had just started, but it seemed as if it was taking all day. Raekwon felt sick to his stomach, and his body was aching from all of the action. He was just glad he had escaped whatever drug charges they had on Tone and Ben.

Through the cage that separated the front seat of the police car from the back, a voice echoed over the police radio.

"Whitaker to unit two-ten."

The officer in the passenger seat responded, "This is two-ten. Go 'head."

"Put him over there with the rest of them!" Whitaker's voice lingered in the car like a bad odor.

"Roger!" The officer's voice rang in Raekwon's ears like an alarm clock.

Raekwon was waiting to wake up from this dream, but he never did. This was really happening, and there was nothing he could do to stop it.

CHAPTER 14

Raekwon woke up the next morning to the sound of the food tray hatch being opened by the sheriff. "Time for your morning meal," he said in a voice that emphasized the fact that he didn't care whether Raekwon ate or not.

Raekwon uncurled his body from the fetal position and sat up on the bed to slide on the plastic-bottom karate shoes that he was issued. He got up and grabbed the breakfast, which was barely enough to feed a child in grade school. There were a couple of spoonfuls of cornflakes, one boiled egg, a small container of apple juice, and just enough milk to wet the cereal. He was too worried to have an appetite. So, he just drank the swallow of juice.

Raekwon was dressed in a disposable light blue jumpsuit. The cell smelled like piss and paint mixed together. It was empty of everything except for a metal toilet, sink, and a metal sleeping rack with a two-inch thick beanbag mattress.

He paced back and forth nervously while trying to figure out the scope of what was going on. He didn't want to speculate himself to death, but he couldn't stop the worst of thoughts from penetrating deep inside his conscience.

"Hey police!" a familiar voice yelled a couple of cells down from his.

Raekwon walked up to the door and stared out of the small window. He could see the sheriff, but none of the cells were in his sight to see who it was yelling.

"What you want?" the sheriff answered through the echoing pod.

"When they gonna take me to court?" the voice asked.

The sheriff's voice echoed, "If you came in with the round up yesterday, you got court in thirty minutes."

It finally registered in Raekwon's head that Mondo was the one yelling through his door.

Raekwon lay on the floor and yelled under it, "Hey, Mondo!"

"Who that?" he responded, seeming to be inquisitive.

"Dis Kwon, nigga."

"Shut the fuck up!" a voice yelled from a cell on the top tier. "I'm trying to sleep up here!"

"Fuck you!" Mondo yelled back at the man, who didn't respond. "Hey Kwon!" he called.

"What's up?

"Uhh, uh, where that nigga Tone at?" Mondo asked in a skeptical manner.

"I don't know. I was gonna ask you the same thang."

"I went by his house and his shit was kicked in." Raekwon assured Mondo that Tone had been arrested, too.

Thirty minutes seemed like two hours, but the time to go to court finally came. The sun was just starting to rise. The glare fought its way through the blurry jail cell window.

The sheriff opened the hatch. "Come on, youngster. It's time for court".

Raekwon walked up to the door and turned around so his back would be facing the cell's entrance. He put his hands behind his back through the hatch opening to let the sheriff place the handcuffs on him.

The sheriff began putting the cuffs around his wrists. "You done got yourself in a big mess, huh, youngster?"

Raekwon looked over his left shoulder and through the window of the cell door. "What you mean?" He was nervous but didn't show it.

"They got the big boys out there waiting to take a couple of you stupid fucks to court. We don't see the U.S. marshals around here much unless it's something big." The sheriff let out a 'you're fucked' giggle.

Raekwon didn't bother to respond to the sarcastic bastard because it served no purpose. He was in a vulnerable situation already and didn't want to add any fuel to the fire. All he wanted to do was make a phone call.

He stepped inside of the van, shackled to Mondo. Meko and Tone were already sitting inside. Everybody looked surprised to see each other.

"Where was y'all niggas at?" Raekwon asked.

"Shit, we was on the other side in building B," Tone answered emotionless.

Tone told them that they didn't have enough evidence to convict them. He said they were trying to use them to get more evidence on him.

"Don't let these muthafuckas trick y'all wit' this bullshit. They just trying to break y'all niggas down and make y'all tell on me."

Raekwon lived by the code of the streets and would take every transaction he had ever made to his grave. He'd never been a rat, and he wasn't going to compromise his morals just because he was in a vulnerable situation. He had heard a lot about the Feds. He heard about how some niggas had even snitched on their closest of family members. If a man doesn't fear you, he's capable of doing against you.

The drive to the courthouse was unbelievable. Raekwon couldn't understand what he was seeing. The marshals of the transport van wore bulletproof vests. The one in the passenger seat had a fully loaded machine gun, and there were four unmarked who had fully loaded machine guns, as well. There were four unmarked vehicles with federal government license plates. One led the way, while the other three drove along the sides and back of the van. A helicopter took the sky.

They made it appear as if they had some of the most dangerous mobsters on the face of the earth in custody. The highway traffic cleared the path for the government vehicles to pass. The onlookers' eyes were glued to the infamous appearance of the innocent until proven guilty, which was them.

The arraignment took no longer than ten minutes. The judge asked them if they understood their rights, read off their charges from the indictments, and then they were hauled off to a federal holding facility afterwards.

Raekwon and Meko were assigned to the opposite unit of Tone and Mondo. Raekwon immediately knew that the Feds were trying to divide and conquer them. It was an obvious thing to figure out that they wanted Tone and Mondo to think Raekwon and Meko would turn against them since they were the youngest.

When Raekwon got in the unit, he went straight to the phone and called his mother collect.

"Hello," Roxanne answered. After the telephone recording gave her the option to accept or reject the call, she accepted it. "You done really got yourself in some mess this time, didn't you?"

"They makin' it seem worse than it really is." Raekwon defended himself, knowing there wasn't much evidence on him.

"Ben just turned himself in dis mornin'. He came runnin' ova here to my house wit' a briefcase full of money, tellin' me to take half of it to his lawyer. That man scared the devil out of me."

"Oh yeah?" Raekwon replied.

"Yeah, boy. They had his face on the news and everything. I ain't neva seen that man scared like that in all my years of knowing him." She emphasized the fact of how shaken up Ben was and continued. "Uhh, boy, you know that silly gal of yours, Portia, won't stop callin' over here at my house."

Raekwon sucked his teeth. "What she talking 'bout?"

"Boy, that gal worried to death 'bout you," Roxanne told him. "She keep callin' and asking me if I done heard from you yet.

"I'm 'bout to call her real quick to let her know where they got me at. Alright, Mom?"

"Alright then, boy. You be strong now and I love you."

"Alright, Mom. I love you, too."

Immediately after they hung up, hHe dialed Portia's number. After five rings, she finally answered.

"Hello." Her voice had a little energy to it.

"What's wrong wit' you, girl? You sound like you got somethin' on yo' mind," Raekwon said, noticing that something was bothering her.

"Man, I'm just tired of going through this. I guess you think I'm one of them stupid girls or somethin'."

"What you mean I think you stupid?"

Portia snapped. "Nigga, just what I said! You musta thought I wasn't gonna find out about that bitch Shae, huh? I ain't even have to go try to find out either 'cause you left yo' pager in my car. I wasn't gonna call back, but since you went to jail and the muthafucka wouldn't stop beepin', I called to see who it was and the dumb bitch told me everything. Oooo, I can't—"

"Hold up, girl. Hold up," Raekwon said, trying to explain. "That bitch is lyin'. I ain't fuck wit' that bitch!"

"How the fuck she get yo' pager number then?"

He lied again, "I don't know."

Portia sighed. "See, that's what I mean right there. You think I'm stupid. Why you keep lyin' to me?"

"Girl, I ain't lyin'. You need to stop listenin' to these punk-ass hoes. You know they just hatin'."

Raekwon was lying his ass off. He knew that she knew, but he wasn't going to give in.

Portia screamed into the phone, "I hate you!" Then, she hung up in his face.

He didn't even bother to call back because he knew it wouldn't do any good. Portia was fed up with him at this point. He could hear it in her voice, and with him being in jail, it wasn't going to make the situation any better.

The unit was loud with people of all races. It was a small unit with very few activities. Raekwon could just look around and figure out it was designed to make a prisoner think a lot, until he broke all the way down.

He walked down the stairs to the bottom tier, where Meko was sitting in a chair outside of his cell smoking a cigarette. He was talking to a short, stocky, dark-skinned dude.

Raekwon walked up to Meko and said, "Nigga, let me get one of them squares."

"Nigga, stop playing. Now you know damn well you don't smoke no cigarettes.

"Shit, I'm 'bout to start right here today. A nigga stressed out. My bitch is tripping and some mo' shit."

The fella Meko had been talking to nodded his head at Raekwon. "What's happenin', man? My name is Ced, homie." He extended his hand.

"I'm Raekwon, homie," he responded, shaking his hand.

Ced said, "Like I was telling ya boy Meko, if y'all need anything, let me know. I know how it is when a nigga first get here, so I be tryin' to look out for a few when I can."

It was cool to meet somebody with some hospitality. Most dudes didn't give a fuck if a nigga needed something or not. It was every man for himself. Ced turned out to be a cool dude, and the three of them spent a lot of time conversing. Ced was older, humble, and very knowledgeable.

After about a week, Meko got released on bond. The Feds didn't want to give Raekwon a bond because they knew he was close to Tone.

The months seemed to get longer and longer as each one passed. Every time they went to court, they sat and listened to the lawyers and prosecutors speak what seemed like a language Raekwon couldn't understand.

He was lying in his cell studying the dictionary. The unexpected appearance of the guard looking in Raekwon's cell window surprised him. He sat up on the bed.

The guard opened the door and said, "You have a legal visit."

Raekwon didn't understand why his lawyer would be coming to see him. He didn't have to go to court again for another month or so. He was a little nervous because he didn't know if the news he had for him was going to be good news or bad.

When Raekwon stepped into the lawyer-client visiting room, his lawyer stood up and shook his hand. He was a tall, lanky Jewish man with a full beard. Jonathan Abbadah was very knowledgeable of the law. He had his way of making Raekwon think he was fighting his hardest fight for him so he wouldn't have a reason to fire him.

Raekwon sat down in a chair across the table from Mr. Abbadah as he scanned some documents he had pulled from his briefcase. He twirled his ink pen around with his fingers and looked Raekwon in the eyes.

"I have some good news and I have some bad news. Which one would you like to hear first?"

Raekwon hesitated for a moment before he said, "Tell me the good news first so the bad news won't be as bad."

"Okay. Well, the good news is that you have a good chance at getting a bond because I filed a motion to dismiss on grounds that you weren't granted a fair speedy trail. The government doesn't want that. I discussed it with the prosecutor, and they would be willing to not object to your bond if we agree to not follow through with our speedy trail motion.

Raekwon nodded to show that he understood what he was saying. "How good is the chance for it to be dismissed?" he asked with interest.

"Well, I wouldn't get my hopes up for the dismissal if I were you," Mr. Abbadah replied. "This judge is very critical of those types of issues, and it's his call. I figured it would be a good chance to get you out on bond. So what you want to do?"

Raekwon sat for a minute in contemplation. It was a hard decision to make knowing that he wanted so badly for the charges to be dismissed against him. He figured Mr. Abbadah knew what the judge's decision would be better than he would.

"Uh, just do the thing with the bond 'cause I don't want to take no chances trying to gamble."

"Okay, I'll get on that right away," his attorney replied, looking down at one of the several documents that lay in front of him. "Oh, and by the way, I also found out that your step-father had been a holdover in the county jail and he made bond."

Raekwon grew tense because the bad news was on its way to his plate. He had to eat it whether he wanted to or not, so he prepared himself for the unexpected.

Mr. Abbadah fixed his posture and cleared his voice. "Okay, now the bad news doesn't affect you so much, but your name did come up. Are you familiar with an Armondo Fletcher?"

"Yeah, I know who he is. He's on our case." Raekwon stroked his chin.

The attorney sat his ink pen on the table. "Well, he's cooperated with the government. He's got a shitload of incriminating things to say about Tone Ashley. Here in these documents that I obtained, he's only spoken of you as being a drug worker of Tone's who he's heard from Tone that you purchase quantities of drugs from Tone in ounces. That can't really hurt you unless he says he's seen you buy the drugs."

Raekwon was shocked by the information. At that point, it all came back to him why he always felt a bad aura whenever he was around Mondo. Those were the type of niggas who would turn on you. The bad thing about it was that he knew too much about Tone.

Raekwon asked his lawyer for a copy of every document before he left the visit. He had mixed feelings, and that's just what good and bad news mixed together did to a person.

Raekwon sat on the documents he received from his lawyer for a couple of days. Finally, he had a chance to send word to Tone that he was going to leave something in between a book in the law library that he needed to see. When shit finally hit the fan, the direction of everything changed instantly. Everybody involved with their case loss hope. Their chances of beating the case were slim to none. Mondo was sent to wait it out in a county jail.

The months seemed like they were passing by slow. Shae and a couple of other people had written Raekwon letters, but he never wrote back. He hadn't called and talked to anybody because he knew it would discourage him. Wanting to check up on everybody, he built up the energy to call his brother Tip.

Tip picked up the phone after two rings. "Hello."

"What's up, nigga?"

Tip answered, "What's up, my nigga? I ain't heard from you in a while, lil' bro. I hope you keepin' yo' head up in there, 'cause that shit gonna be over soon."

Raekwon sighed. "Yeah, I hope so. Shit, what you been up to?" He quickly changed the subject to temporarily free his mind.

"Man," Tip's voice got low, "I be stayin' out the way. Niggas done gone crazy out here. You know them niggas Kel and Carlos is locked up, fightin' a murder case."

That was unbelievable news to him. "Oh yeah? What happened?"

Tip paused for a moment. "Shit, man, I don't really know the whole story or if the shits even true. All I know is that the police picked them niggas up a couple of days ago."

Raekwon sighed. "Damn, man, that shit's crazy."

"Hell yeah, that's what I said when I heard it. Uh, Kel's lil' cousin, Bebe, got shot in the head a couple of weeks ago. He's in a wheelchair 'cause his balance is fucked up. They say he got into it with the nigga Kemo. That's who they say did it, but you know how niggas is. They don't be knowin' a lot of shit to the story fa' sho'."

Raekwon said, "Yeah, nigga, you got to be careful out there, 'cause I'll go crazy if somethin' happen to you."

"I just been stayin' in the house 'cause niggas is on some other shit. Shit ain't been the same since you left."

"I'm 'bout to get off this phone, my nigga, so tell everybody I said what's up."

"Alright then. I can't wait 'til you get out," Tip said sympathetically before they hung up.

Raekwon spent his days and nights worried about what would happen to him. He was worried about what would happen in Kel and Carlos' situation, also. He was stressed out and started to sleep a lot.

The environment was fucked up. A bunch of miserable niggas walking around with a chip on their shoulders, and he was one of them. The day finally came when he got the bond he had been waiting for, and he felt like half the world was lifted from off his shoulders.

CHAPTER 15

It had been two months since Raekwon had gotten out on bond. Things were moving as slow as he had ever seen them move for him. Life seemed worse than it had ever before been. Raekwon was paranoid of the Feds and felt like they were watching every move he made. There was no way on God's green earth that he was going to pick up another sack of crack.

Day in and day out, he drove through the streets of The Maze and felt the stroke of the struggler's hands sliding down his back. He got a petty job just so he would be able to rent an apartment in the Crossings. He couldn't believe how broke he was. Portia had left him a couple of months after he got locked up, and the game had grown into another phase since then.

Raekwon stepped outside of his apartment and walked to the parking lot to get inside his car. Just before he could reach in his pocket to grab the keys and unlock the door, he noticed some sprinkles of glass on the ground by his back tire. He grew suspicious and walked towards the back of the car.

"What the—" he yelled.

His back windshield had a hole through it the size of his head. He shook his head and sighed. He was furious inside. Raekwon grabbed an old towel out of his trunk so he could wipe the glass off his backseat. When he opened the back door, he noticed a folded piece of paper laying next to the brick that had been lodged into his window.

What in the hell is this? he thought.

He picked up the paper and unfolded it. Written across the page in large letters were the words *Die, Bitch! Die!* He stroked his chin as he stared at the handwriting. Something about it looked familiar, but it seemed that whoever wrote it thought they were being intelligent by purposely writing sloppy.

"That's whose shit this look like," he said out loud.

Raekwon remembered some letters that Shae had written to him. When he never bothered to write her back, she started to send hate letters, but he just brushed it off as something simple. He was now starting to put everything together. *This bitch done forgot to cross her T's and dot her I's one too many muthafuckin' times,* he thought and began nodding.

Raekwon couldn't remember Shae's phone number if his life depended on it. He sat in the driver's seat of his car, holding his cell phone in one hand and massaging his temple with the other.

"Fuck it. I don't wanna call the bitch anyway. I'ma just pop up on her stank ass," he said, while started up his car and gritting his teeth.

He pulled up to the Sierra Vistas. Raekwon hated the fact that it was broad daylight because there was no telling what he was capable of doing to the bitch. He was driving around with a broken window, and he was mad about it, too.

Raekwon stood in front of Shae's apartment and knocked for about five minutes. He had his poker face on and was ready to confront her. Suddenly, he noticed the next door neighbor's door opening.

A nappy-headed, dark-skinned broad stuck her head out of the door. "Ain't no sense in you wastin' no mo' of yo' time standin' there knockin' 'cause that gal got evicted last month sometime." Her buck teeth showed when she talked.

"Oh yeah?" he asked surprisingly.

"Umm, huh," she said, as a little boy ran out into the hall with nothing on but some piss-stained cartoon character underwear. The lady stepped out into the hall and smacked the little boy on the side of his head. "Boy, if you don't get yo' ass back in there, I swear I'ma... just go now!" she yelled.

"A'ight. Good lookin' out." He walked off.

He hopped in the car and got into traffic. He was on his way back to town when he remembered Shae's dad lived around the corner form Silverman Park.

"Aw, yeah," he said and slammed his hand down on the steering wheel with a closed first.

He didn't want to be obvious. He had to see if she was even over there. Her dad was a big, black-ass, crazy dude that didn't like for niggas to be at his house. Raekwon wasn't going to take the chance at letting him get his hands on him because that's when things would get really ugly for everybody involved.

Raekwon drove by the street and looked to see if her pop's van was there. It was gone. He came back around the block and down the street. Noticing the door was open, he stopped in front of the house and honked the horn.

One of Shae's friends, Brenda, looked out the window. Raekwon immediately hopped out of his car, leaving it running in the middle of the street with the door wide open. He walked up to the house and knocked several times. When nobody came to the door, he knocked harder.

Shae finally appeared with Brenda walking behind her. They both had bandannas tied around their heads, looking just like the ghetto hoodrats they were.

Shae opened the screen door with an innocent looking smile. "What's up, boy? How you been doin'?" she asked, acting like things were normal.

Raekwon gave her a cold stare. "What the fuck you mean, how I been doin'?" He raised his left eyebrow and laced his fingers together. "Why you fuck up my shit?"

Shae gave a light smirk. "What shit you talkin' 'bout?"

He knew she was playing stupid just because of the smirk that she was trying to hide. He felt like she was trying to play him for a lame-ass dude.

Raekwon snapped. "Bitch, you know what shit I'm talking about! You broke my muthafuckin' window on my car!" he yelled.

"Nigga, I ain't yo' muthafuckin' bitch, and that's what the fuck you get!" Shae popped back at him slick, while shifting her head back and forth as if she was rolling her eyes.

POP! Raekwon smacked the shit out of her and then stepped back off the porch and into the front yard. "Bitch, bring yo' punk ass outside!" he demanded.

Shae rushed towards him, screaming and swinging. He grabbed her by the neck and threw her on the ground and into the dirt. He wanted to break the broad's face, but he somehow managed to keep himself slightly in control. His adrenaline was rushing like he had drunk ten cups of coffee.

"Punk-ass nigga, get your hands off—" Brenda said while trying to rush Raekwon from behind.

Raekwon threw Brenda on top of Shae while Shae was trying to get up.

"Mind yo' muthafuckin' business, bitch!" He started looking around in rage for the first weapon in his sight. He spotted the water hose and quickly made his way towards it.

Shae started running towards Raekwon. By now, he had the water hose in both of his hands. He wrapped the hose around her neck. As he was slinging her across the yard, Brenda jumped on Raekwon's back and hit him over the head with a closed fist.

"You lil' punk-ass bitch. I'll beat yo' ass if—"

Raekwon threw Brenda over his shoulder and kicked her in the ass when she landed on the ground. He was breathing like the police were chasing him. He couldn't even finish saying what he was going to tell her.

Shae ran towards the front door and Brenda was right behind her. Raekwon wasn't satisfied, but there wasn't much he could do to two helpless broads that didn't stand a chance. He didn't like hitting on females, but his blind rage took control of that situation.

"Bitch, what you 'bout to do, call the police on a nigga or something?" he asked sarcastically, throwing the hose to the ground.

Out of breath, she spat back, "Nigga, you should've neva put yo' muthafuckin' hands on me. I'ma have my cousin Sabastian whoop yo' muthafuckin' ass. As a matter of fact, I'm 'bout to go call him now."

"Fuck that nigga, bitch! Call him! I ain't hard to find."

The neighbors were standing in their yards and looking out of their windows. He didn't care who was looking, though. That's how mad he was.

"And yeah, yo' punk ass gonna pay for breakin' out my muthafuckin' window. You owe me for slicing my tires, too. I know you did that shit, bitch!"

Noticing that he had traffic backed up, Raekwon walked to his car to pull over in front of her house, but Shae slammed the front door after calling him a bitch-ass nigga. The brick that was in his backseat, he threw it through their front window, hopped in his car, and sped off.

When he pulled up to Bodine's house, there were quite a few people standing outside. There was always a house full of dudes over there. His mother didn't really trip, as long as whenever somebody went to the liquor store, they brought her a beer back.

Black Eddy stepped away from the car that he was leaning on in the driveway. "What's up, my nigga?"

Raekwon gave him a half hug. He hadn't seen Black Eddy in a while. He had just gotten acquitted for murder. The rumors was on the streets had almost got him convicted for the death of Magic.

Bodine was sitting on the porch smoking on a blunt. One of his sisters was harassing him, trying to hit the weed. "Get the fuck away from me, girl. You got yo' own muthafuckin' weed." He cut his eyes at her and picked up his beer.

There was a couple of dudes shooting dice on the side of the house. "Nigga, I put that twenty down. Don't fuck wit' my shit!" one of them yelled.

Bodine yelled from the porch, "Y'all niggas gonna have to take that shit somewhere else if y'all gonna be arguing and shit."

Raekwon leaned back on the front of the old bucket that was parked in the driveway. He was watching the dice game, contemplating if he was going to hop in it or not. Raekwon decided to keep his limited supply of money in his pocket. Things were rough for him now that he wasn't selling dope.

Black Eddy walked up and stood next to Raekwon. He tapped him on the arm and leaned over into his ear. "Hey, nigga, let a muthafucka buy one of them quarter birds you got stashed."

Raekwon looked at him like he was crazy. "Nigga, I don't fuck wit' that shit no mo'. You really tryin' to see a nigga get sent up the river somewhere, huh?"

"Stop playin', Kwon. I know you ain't got scared all of a sudden." He looked at Raekwon as if he was bullshitting.

"I don't know what you looking at me like that for. Shit, the Feds ain't playin wit' niggas, man. They already tryin' to hang a muthafucka." Raekwon sighed. They probably followin' me around as we speak." Raekwon gave him a serious look.

Black Eddy scanned the street with curiosity. "Man, fuck that. I gotta get money. I got too many kids to feed, and I ain't gonna be walkin' around this muthafucka lookin' like no bum."

In a way, Raekwon felt just like he did. It was all he really knew how to do, but for some natural reason, the Feds had him paranoid. He was thankful that he wasn't at the top of the totem pole on Tone's case. He had sat in jail with niggas who were facing thirty and forty years for some kilos the Feds had never found. That was enough to make a blind man see. Every time Raekwon got tempted, he thought about how niggas had forgotten about him when he was locked up.

Hrrrrat! Hrrrrat! Hrrat! The sounds of an automatic came out of nowhere. Raekwon had a flashback of his acid trip when the toy Uzi seemed to come to life. The only problem this time was the gun wasn't a toy, and he wasn't the one behind the trigger.

Everybody hit the floor yelling for everybody else to get down. Raekwon was frantic as his chin bounced off of the cemented driveway when he dove to the ground. He blacked out after the dark-colored compact car with no license plate faded up the block at full speed.

Raekwon's mind seemed as if it was fading away with the voices that were in the background. His sweat was heavy, and his heartbeat was all he could hear in his descending conscience. He realized he had just experienced an anxiety attack after he finally heard the screams of Bodine's mother. Raekwon's eyes opened, and he took a deep breath.

"Who just shot my baby?" Bodine's mother screamed at the top of her lungs after rushing outside to see what had happened. The look on her face was somewhere between life and death.

Raekwon quickly got up off of the ground and ran over to where Bodine's sister lay dying in the front yard. He gasped and shook his head in shame. He was speechless.

Bodine's mother held her daughter's motionless body in her arms and cried out, "Somebody call the fucking ambulance! All of y'all just get the fuck away from me!"

Raekwon walked off towards his car. He wanted to give the family some space. A tear rolled down his cheek. He was thinking about revenge, but the only way was to know who had done the drive-by.

He stopped in the middle of the street and turned around. Bodine was leaning up against the house with his face buried in the palms of his hands. One thing he noticed was that everybody who had been present before the shooting took place was still present, except for Black Eddy. His car was gone.

Later on that night, Raekwon sat in his apartment alone. The TV was on, but he was staring right through it, deep in his thoughts. There was an empty beer bottle sitting on the coffee table beside a bag of potato chips.

He had on nothing but a pair of jeans. His stomach growled. He looked at his out-of-shape gut without gaining an appetite.

Raekwon picked up the remote control and turned up the volume as a newsbreak flashed across the screen. He was alarmed at what he was seeing.

He sighed and asked himself, "What the fuck this nigga done did?" Raekwon then gave the TV his undivided attention.

What he ended up finding out on the news was that Black Eddy had gotten arrested for gunning down two men at a restaurant in broad daylight. Raekwon got up and paced the living room. He couldn't seem to control his rage. He punched a hole in one of the living room walls and then lay down across the couch biting his fingernails until he dozed off.

The next day, he drove through town paranoid. He was paranoid that the police might've been looking for him to ask him some questions that he wasn't going to answer. He wasn't sure, but that was the guess of his wandering mind.

Raekwon passed by The Market and saw Kel's cousin Babe flagging him down from the parking lot. He was in his wheelchair and had a blank look on his face.

Raekwon pulled up next to Babe. "Nigga, what the fuck you doin' up here in yo' wheelchair? Nigga, you on some bullshit," he said angrily.

Raekwon could see where Babe's head had been opened and a metal plate placed inside. Just by observing his demeanor, it seemed like he had grown into a young nigga of a thousand struggles overnight.

Babe reached in his pocket, pulling out a five-dollar bill. "Nigga. suh, suh, sell me a blunt, fool," he stuttered.

Raekwon looked at him in shame. "Nigga, I ain't got no weed, and if I did, I wouldn't sell you shit. You need to have yo' ass at home somewhere."

After a long conversation due to his uncontrollable stuttering, Bebe told Raekwon that Carlos and Kel had gotten tried in separate trials. He said Carlos beat the case yesterday, but Kel had gone to trail first and was found guilty. Bebe said they were trying to sentence Kel to life in prison.

What Raekwon had just heard didn't really register until he pulled off. He felt a sharp pain in his stomach when he thought about Kel. His childhood friend had just been convicted of several murders.

Raekwon couldn't think past the bad news. He pulled over at a park and lit up a cigarette. He took long, uneasy drags, filling his car up with so much smoke that he had to roll down the windows.

He picked up his cell phone and dialed Carlos' number.

"Hello," his mother answered in a skeptical voice.

"Can I speak to Carlos?" Raekwon sounded concerned.

"Who is this?" she asked suspiciously.

"This is Kwon."

"Kwon? How did you know he was here?" She sounded like he was the last person she wanted to hear from.

He hesitated. "Uh, I heard that Carlos was out, so I was just calling to see how he was doing."

"Okay, I'll let you talk to him this time, but I don't want any of you guys calling here anymore."

She put Carlos on the phone.

"What's up, man?" Carlos sounded uninterested.

"What's up, my nigga? How you doing?"

"I'm cool," he responded with no emotion.

Raekwon began to have an uneasy feeling about how he was responding. He got a sense that his mother was somehow blaming him for what Carlos went through. Maybe she thought he was a bad choice for a friend.

Raekwon asked, "How come yo' moms don't want a nigga to call no more?"

Carlos sighed. "Shit, she trippin', man. Some niggas shot up the house last night after I got home from beatin' that case. I don't know who it was, but they had me sleepin' wit' my pistol.

"Oh yeah?" Raekwon asked, concerned.

"Yeah, man. That shit got my mom scared, homie. To tell you the truth, I'm scared, too," he explained, but this time with emotion. "My mom is moving. She wants to move out of town."

"Fuck it, homie. I think that it'll be the best thing for you to do. Where you movin' to?" Raekwon asked.

"I don't even know yet, man. I can't trust nobody. I woke up in the middle of the night sweatin' 'bout that. I'll try to get in touch wit' you to let you know. If nobody else knows, you'll know.

Raekwon was kind of sad. "A'ight then, my nigga. Don't forget to holla at a muthafucka, man."

Carlos agreed and hung up.

Everything was falling apart. Raekwon didn't know what to do with himself. It was a trip how everyone had grown apart. Too much crazy stuff was happening for him to keep his lips from taking him to the bottom of a liquor bottle. He drank himself to sleep every night for two weeks.

***

He was driving slowly. Not because he wanted to, but because he had to. This was the second funeral he was attending within two months. Raylin had gotten shot in the chest seven times by some nigga from out of town. The word was they robbed him at a dope spot.

Raekwon trailed the long line of cars with his headlights on. They followed the black limos and the hearse to the burial site.

Tip was in the car with Raekwon, but they rode in silence. It sure wasn't a ride to enjoy because it was filled with pain. Raekwon reminisced about the many good times he and Raylin had shared while they were growing up. He and Raylin got their first piece of pussy together the summer before they started seventh grade.

Sometimes after the police had raided Raylin's mother's house and charged him with possessing a controlled substance, Raekwon told him that he needed to slow down and that he couldn't cop his dope from him no more. They fell out after that conversation because Raylin felt like Raekwon was trying to tell him what to do. Raekwon just didn't want to have dealings with him while he was out on bond on a drug charge. His mother's house almost got taken away from her because of her son's wrongdoings. But, he didn't want to listen. He started copping from anyone that had it, and there were consequences that followed.

Before Raylin's casket was lowered into the ground, the preacher read a scripture from the bible. Proverbs 18:21 says that death and life are in the power of the tongue, and they that love it shall eat the fruit thereof. The preacher then told them to bow their heads as he prayed.

Raekwon paid his last respects. Everything he wanted to say to Raylin rolled down his face and dropped into the cemetery soil by message of the couple of tears he shed. Whoever said that men weren't supposed to cry lied to the world. He thought about what his mother had told them. She had wanted to go, but she wouldn't be able to bear it because it felt like one of her sons had died. It was just too close to the family.

The town had fallen apart in more ways than one. Raekwon thought that a lot of niggas had found peace elsewhere because he never saw or heard from them. It was different than it was before.

Raekwon was living a life that didn't seem normal. He was sending money to Tone, Black Eddy, and Kel whenever he was able to. There was the fact that he was struggling, and he had a lot of sleepless nights.

Every time he drove through town, Raekwon saw another generation that would have to learn things the hard way. Kel's little cousin Bebe was part of the generation. Ever since he had recovered enough to walk again, he had gone wild.

Raekwon got word that Bebe incited a shootout at a house party that ended up claiming the life of Kel's younger brother. Bebe was shot again in the hip. By the way Kel reacted to hearing about the whole situation, it seemed as if he didn't know if he was dead or alive himself.

Things got foul concerning the dope case that Raekwon was fighting. Ben snitched on him to get himself out of the mess that he made. He had caught another dope case while he was on bond, and the pressure that the Feds put on him busted every pipe that his reputation ever laid.

Raekwon was shattered by the information his lawyer had given him. He now knew what it felt like to have a person that basically raised him turn their back on him. This was something he had never imagined to happen in a thousand years. It felt like a sharp rod had gotten shoved into his back and right through the middle of his heart.

Turning himself in would be the hard part. He wanted to flee, but he didn't want to be on the run. He was drained physically and emotionally. The only sleep he was able to get was when his body would completely shut down on him. He didn't want to miss out on a damn thing, so he drowned himself in the nightlife.

Roxanne helped her son realize there was nothing but trouble in the streets, and he didn't need to be digging a bigger hole to fall into. Sooner or later, the day would come for him to face the music no matter what he chose to do. Raekwon didn't want to, but he threw in the towel and turned himself in, becoming defenseless and vulnerable.

CHAPTER 16

Prison was everything Raekwon expected it to be. It provided every disappointment that a man would ever try to avoid. His hands were tied behind his back, figuratively. There was nothing he could do from this position. Who would listen to him now? He was out of reach and out of touch.

Raekwon was just another number added to the inmate population. A psychological design that was created to make a person institutionalized. The struggle was far beyond his understanding. In order to understand, he had to observe and endure the inevitable pain that followed.

Some days went by slow and some fast, but they all went just the same, miserable. In order to keep his sanity, he had to accept his situation as it was and push forward. Seconds became minutes, minutes became hours, and hours became days. Before he knew it, he was over a thousand days.

He strolled through the prison halls that were full of dust and odor. He was on his way back to his cell to read the letter he had just received from Kel, who he hadn't heard from in over three years.

As he walked, the roar of his voice rang through every corner of the human warehouse. There were samples of conversations that ranged from sports to women, and money to drama. Raekwon didn't get himself involved with most of the dudes that were around him because they thought they had so much game and that someone wouldn't be able to recognize their motives. Most of them were only out to get you to hook them up with a broad.

"Hurry up and lay the muthafuckin' domino, nigga!" a skinny, light-skinned dude started. "Nigga, you ain't take that long to hop on that muthafuckin' fifteen-year deal them white folks slapped across your face."

"Nigga, fuck you! Domino, you half-breed bastard! Count that shit up!" a buff, dark-skinned inmate with a perm responded.

Raekwon gave a light laugh as he passed by the two who were playing a sensitive game of dominoes. This was the type of stuff he heard every day. He was burnt out on seeing the same faces and hearing the same shit, but he had to do his time like a soldier.

When Raekwon finally made it to his cell, he went inside and sat down on his bed. He looked at the front of the envelope and sighed. He was happy to hear from Kel, but he was sad to entertain the thought that he would never be able to walk the streets again. It seemed like it took forever to open the letter, but he finally got it open. He unfolded the letter and started to read it.

Dear Kwon,

What's up, my nigga? It's been a while since a nigga been able to holler at you, homie. I got yo' hook up from that nigga

Dre. All this time they gave me is killin' a nigga. I still can't believe I got a life sentence, man. I just can't accept this shit. They got me in here fucked up off of this Prozac shit 'cause I be trippin' out. I'm trying to keep my head up and hold on, but it's hard when a nigga can't see no light and ain't got no support. Niggas that was so-called homies ain't sent me one red cent to survive off of. Niggas won't even respond to my letters or even get the block off they phone so I can call. Fuck everybody, though. I see how it is. All niggas is showing me is that I ain't got no real friends. I miss you, though, my nigga, and I bet them niggas is treatin' you the same way. I know you still gotta finish doin' your time, but at least you know that you getting out one day soon. Muthafuckas don't even care about me now that they ain't around me. Out of sight, out of mind.

Nigga, my lil' brother done got killed out there in the streets, and I'm numb now. I guess that shit came back on me. I knew my pops was stressed out, but my people told me that the nigga been smoking that shit, and I can't seem to understand that one. That ain't even like him, but I guess shit changes. I ain't heard from him in about a year; he just left me for dead. Him and my stepmom got divorced. They wouldn't stop arguing about why my lil' bro died. Why that shit have to happen to him? I ask myself that every day. He was only fourteen, man.

My son gotta grow up without me around now. His mom told me that the kids at his school be teasin' him 'cause they know his dad is in jail. She said he be askin' her when I'm gonna come home. I be just wantin' to cry sometimes, but I'm all drained out, homie.

How good it be feeling just to get a letter from a muthafucka. I got to keep my mind focused on what I gotta do in

243

here, though. This is my home for the rest of my life unless my appeal falls through for me. Until then, I'm stuck.

Write me back, though, my nigga.

One Love,
Kel

Raekwon sat the letter on the desk and lay back on the bed with his hands laced behind his head. It seemed as if he could almost feel the pain that Kel was feeling. Raekwon had his share of experiencing people turning their backs on him, too. He understood why most of the convicts around him had the stare of death in their eyes. To kill or be killed meant nothing when you already felt dead inside.

Raekwon grinned and let out a light snicker. He was remembering the time when he was a juvenile and Kenny asked him where he saw himself in five years. It was now five years later, and he was lying in a prison cell, the one place he would've never thought he was going to be. He was now being challenged to see if he could stay alive in this type of environment because some never made it back out. Raekwon had heard all of the stories about it, and he wasn't trying to be added to the list of non-survivors.

He realized that in order for him to survive, he had to free himself mentally. He knew that whatever goes up must come down, whatever lives must one day die. So, in that same breath, whatever is started must come to an end one day.

He never knew that he was so off track. He lived everyday on the streets like death was near. He was taught to fear none, and that's the only way he knew how to live. Prison was one of man's worst enemies, and Raekwon learned to use his enemies to his own advantages.

He was now able to see the limits and boundaries of people, and how they ended up disappointing him if he trusted and depended on them. Reality is perfect, and nothing is permanent. Through it all, he was glad his mother never kept him blinded from the real struggles of life.

He got up and threw on his government-issued khaki coat and his grey winter hat. Ced wanted him to meet him out on the yard since he decided he wasn't going to the chow hall to get the shit on a shingle that was being served. The four o'clock count had been cleared, and the turnkey had opened up the iron gates.

As Raekwon made his way through the metal detector at the checkpoint, he cut his eyes at the guard who was in charge of that area. He was bitter inside and wasn't happy with the way they talked to and treated them.

"Pull up your fuckin' pants!" the guard yelled.

Raekwon kept his comment to himself because the hole wasn't too far away. He just kept walking without looking back.

The brisk fall breeze had a chill to it, but it wasn't cold. The breath of life floated through the fingers of the tree branches, carrying away the bright-colored leaves that slowly fell to the ground. As he observed nature, he realized how he now appreciated all of the little things he never took time to notice.

When he stepped out on the yard, he glanced at the gun tower for a split second. It had become a habit for him to do that. Raekwon always liked to stay well aware of his surroundings.

Ced was standing by the weight pile talking to a sophisticated-looking white man. Ced was always up to some high-powered stuff. He associated with people from all different races. He always told Raekwon to never think that the niggas had all of the game.

Raekwon had learned a lot from Ced over at the holding facility back when he first caught his case. The Feds hit Ced with ten years for robbing a gun shop that was federally insured. He told Raekwon about so many large robberies that he was too embarrassed to speak on the small licks he had hit in his life. He told Raekwon that most of the niggas that he knew on the streets called him Shovel Loc, because if somebody cheated him out of some money, he would bury it with them.

When Ced noticed Raekwon walking up, he shook the white man's hand and parted ways with him. He walked up to Raekwon and connected closed fists with him.

"What's goin' on wit' you, boy?"

Raekwon gave him an uncertain look. "Nothin' much, just puttin' up with the same bullshit, like always."

Ced looked at Raekwon as if to say he was too young to be stressing. "Come walk a couple of laps around this track wit' me."

They walked in silence. Raekwon stared beyond the six-foot, barb wired fences that surrounded the yard. He could see the existence of life, but in life, he didn't seem to exist. He was numb to pain.

Ced broke the silence after about a minute and a half. "Since you're getting out real soon, what you plan on doin' to get back on your feet?"

"Shit..." Raekwon hesitated for a moment and then

continued. "A nigga gonna try to get that music shit off the ground, if I can."

Ced stopped walking and cut his eyes at him in a doubtful way. "Stop playin', nigga," he said, then started walking again. "Now be realistic. See, you ain't gotta sell dope or rob no banks or none of that type of shit either."

Raekwon looked at him with interest and raised his left eyebrow. "What might this shit you got going consist of?"

Ced stopped, and Raekwon stopped with him. Ced comically looked around as if to see if anybody had their eyes or ears on him.

Then he gave Raekwon a serious look and said, "Now don't get me wrong, 'cause it ain't nothin' that an angel would do, but it's worth it. You know me. I be on some high-tech shit. Don't look back, but did you see that white boy that I was hollerin' at?"

Their walking pace slowed up a little.

Raekwon looked Ced in the eyes curiously and replied, "Yeah."

"Well, dude is in here on a white-collar crime. He knows a couple of business executives that was doin' the same shit that he was doin', but they didn't get caught up on that shit. He said they keeping millions of dollars in the houses and shit." He coughed and cleared his throat. "Now, look here."

"Uh huh," Raekwon said to let him know he was listening.

"See, dude is salty that none of them scary white muthafuckas that he was getting all the money with ain't even thought to send him a postcard since he's been locked up. All of 'em owe him a nice chunk of change, too. Now, he wanna involve me in it 'cause he knows I will have some muthafucka go over there and strip the clothes off of they backs. We done had some intense conversations, and he trust me to get the job done. All I need is a nigga like you that I can depend on to handle that shit for me when you raise up 'cause I still got a few years left." Ced fixed his hat and started stroking his beard. "He got the plug on the fake police and ATF uniforms and all that. It'll just make them muthafuckas think they gettin' busted. Now, are you trying to be a part of this shit or what?"

Raekwon realized he had walked into history with a mugshot of a convict, fighting his deepest temptations. The only truth was that Raekwon wasn't promised anything. For him, it was a blessing just to be able to wake up every morning.

His whole life flashed through his mind. Where did he go wrong? That was something he would never be able to figure out because he was too far gone into his ways. He knew he had an option to do right or do wrong, but was trying to survive and put food in his stomach the only way he knew how considered doing wrong?

Raekwon couldn't see himself starving, but he also couldn't see himself in a position that could lead to him going back to prison either. Life had a cycle that nobody he knew was able to break, so why try to change that? His conscience started eating at his lost hope. Raekwon needed to get his life on track and try to do things the right way.

He just stared at the barb-wired fence and thought. He knew when he got out, he wouldn't have a pot to piss in or even clothes to put on his back. Deep in his heart, he didn't want to lose his focus again. He twisted the hairs of his mustache while staring into his imagination. He gazed at the barb wire and then at Ced.

Raekwon gave him a serious squint, and with deep emphasis, he said, "Count me in, my nigga."

Those five words put Raekwon right back at the beginning of a long, tiring cycle. How could he turn his back on the only life that he knew? There was one way in and no way out. He had to survive by any means necessary.

THE END

ACKNOWLEDGEMENTS

I like to give a special thank you to the people who always inspired me by believing in me. I thank the greatest power alive, GOD, for life, strength, patience, and focus. To my mom, Linda McClure, I love you. You're a queen. To my intelligent son, Nkosi; and his mother, Erica, who helped me see the future in the darkest nights.

One love to my whole family, the biological and the psychological. My big brother Que & my nephew Darius. My little brother Ephraim, Grandma Annie Mae, my aunties, Shirley, Kela, Mae , Joyce Marie. My uncles, Ricky and Eddie Lee. To my first, second, and third cousins, Jamel, Jawan, James, Jamal, June, Malique, Kia, Tanya, Joy, Lil Joe, Quick, Woodie, Main, Randy, Shedra, and Gloria,& Malkia. My psychological family out there running the streets: Adamlo, Trick-E, Ramalo, Lil' Paul, Lil' Bit, Lil' Tor Midnite, C-Real, China, Creech Kelly (serving 116 years in prison), D-Law, Big Sam, Al, Cameron, that nigga Zaboo my mentor, and my other big brother, Cac and his family for treating me like one of their own. My nigga Trav, Ike, H.K, Scrilla, Gregory, Taz, Bryan Jackson, BG, Lil Nate, Trucc, Clicc-D, Lil Yates, K-Roll, LG, Dante Hill, Bory, Aaron, Tyrus, Michael & Dameion Wells, Dirty Ray, Deshaun Becerril, Dirty Swa, Lil K-Dog, Big Boo & Lil Boo, Lil Cyc, Lil Choch, Cossi, Ace

Deuce, Lil P, Ricca, TJ, RJ, The Johnson family, The Law family, The Manuel family, The Sharp family, and my nigga Sharai Hicks.

I know too many people to name, so let my heart defend me on that. To the niggas that I shared a conscious part of my life with in prison, Roc, Pierre, Head Loc, Big D, Tre Hundred, Ash Tre, Man Man, Teflon Ron, Dela, Les, and the real dudes that helped me through my bit. If it weren't for the people that helped me through my bit and the people I know, this wouldn't have been possible.

RIP: Cac the Trendsetta, Charles Culbreath, Andre Price, Lil Wayne, Stephen Johnson, Ms. Mabelle Brooks, Captin Kirk, Ernest Ward, Charles & George Ward, Isaac Johnson (Lil Flash), Mordi ,Mikael Asberry, Preston Hill, Charlis(Lil AK), Kenny Parsons, Grandaddy (McClure), Lil Grandma, Uncle Nute, Stan the man, Sweets, David Harper, Alvin Marshall, Xavier Walker, and my Uncle Sonny. You are all missed.

CHARLES TRUTH

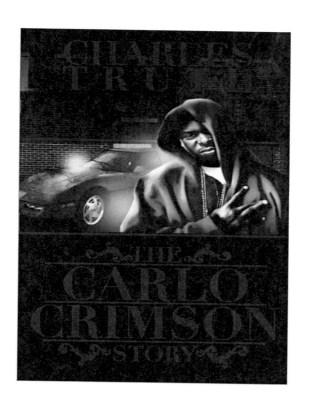

Coming in fall 2011